DRAGON ORB

Firestorm

MARK ROBSON

SIMON AND SCHUSTER

SIMON AND SCHUSTER

First published in Great Britain by Simon and Schuster UK Ltd, 2008
A CBS COMPANY

1 3 5 7 9 10 8 6 4 2

Simon & Schuster UK Ltd
Africa House
64–78 Kingsway
London WC2B 6AH

A CIP catalogue record for this book is
available from the British Library

ISBN 978-1-84738-068-5

Typeset by Rowland Phototypesetting Ltd,
Bury St Edmunds, Suffolk
Printed and bound in Great Britain by
CPI Cox & Wyman Ltd, Reading, Berkshire

*This book is dedicated in particular to the
memory of Captain Albert Ball VC DSO MC,
whose exploits inspired the character of Jack Miller,
and in general to the memory of all the brave 'knights
of the air' who fought with chivalry and honour for
both sides in the Great War.*

Acknowledgements

To April, whose Internet name inspired this
story, and to Brian – a wise old dragon!

To my 'Teen Talk Team': Connor McLean, Esther
Taylor and Janine Brierley, who helped me to hear
the voices of the young dragonriders in this story.

To Mr Peter Murton at the Imperial War
Museum, Duxford, who gave of his time,
his knowledge, and who provided a most
enlightening reading list.

To the National Phobics' Society, and all those
kind individuals who provided me with insights
into irrational fears and Obsessive Compulsive
Disorder.

To the Bishop's Tea Room in Daventry for all the tea and magnificent caramel shortbread that helped inspire me in the mornings.

To Lynne and her team at Middlemore Farm Public House, who allowed me to adopt Table 7 as my 'office' in the afternoons.

Contents

Chapter One

The Devil's Finger

Elian paused to look over his shoulder as he reached the edge of the trees. They were still after him. Sweat trickled in steady rivulets down his forehead, neck and back. He was breathing hard, but his mind was clear: no choice remained – he would have to risk the Devil's Finger. What if they dared to follow? Granted it was unlikely. Like everyone else, Borkas and Farrel were wary of the taboo. But what if they put their fears aside as he had? The thought chilled him to the core. If they did, he would be in big trouble.

Why Borkas and Farrel had chosen to pick on him today was not clear, but he was not about to stop and ask them. None of the local boys were strong enough to stand up to the two thugs. When they had appeared, he had run.

It was strange. Curiosity and a desire for adventure had drawn Elian to the Finger more than a year ago. Daring to go there had felt neither brave nor foolish. Instead he had felt strangely compelled, as if it were a place he was supposed to go. Stories were told of the Devil's Finger in the village; stories designed to keep the youngsters from venturing there. It was a place of dire consequences, they said – a place of death.

On reaching it that first time, Elian had seen the Finger for what it was. Yes, it held danger for the unwary or the foolish, but no more so than many other places along the edge of the Great Escarpment. Sheer drops of up to a thousand spans into the lush green of the Haleen Rift Valley were not uncommon along the edge. The Finger, however, appeared to flout the laws of nature. It was a huge digit of rock projecting from the lip of the sheer cliff that pointed ever eastwards, towards the lands of the rising sun.

He hadn't been through the tangled wood for a while, but an itching sensation at the back of his skull had been plaguing him all week. Memories of his last visit haunted his dreams and thoughts. It felt almost as if the Finger were calling him back – as if he *needed* to visit it. Or was it that *it* needed *him?* With the burly figures of Borkas and Farrel closing fast, any worries about the curious instinct were forgotten. He had come too far to turn back. It was the Finger, or a beating.

He turned and entered the woods. The path was barely distinguishable from the rest of the wild, untamed land near the edge of the Great Escarpment. Tangled briars tore at his boots and the lower branches of the trees clawed at his tunic and hair with gnarled fingers. Driven forwards by need and fear, he ignored them. When he finally broke free from the clutches of the trees he was scratched, tired, and beginning to wonder if this had been such a good idea.

He took a few steps forwards onto the base of the Finger. The cloud seemed little more than a few spans above his head. He drew a deep breath and held it for a moment. The view from the rocky outcrop was one that the Creator had otherwise reserved for the birds. The sense of awe he had felt on his previous visits enveloped him once more with the soft touch of a rich man's cloak.

Elian had never been afraid of heights, but this was one place where he could begin to understand what it must be like to suffer vertigo. He walked forwards further to where the Finger narrowed to a mere couple of paces wide. He was not so foolish as to walk all the way to the tip, for there was no telling how stable such a narrow point of rock might be.

For many, to look down from where he was standing would simply be too much. Some would freeze, unable to move. Others would drop to their hands and knees and crawl back to the safety of the main escarpment. Others still would lie down, close their eyes and beg for someone to save them. It was a curious phenomenon, the fear of heights.

A sudden whoosh of air from behind made Elian drop to one knee for fear of being swept over the edge. As the unexpected gust died with a fading sigh, he slowly rose to his feet. To his horror, he realised he was no longer alone. He could feel a presence behind him. The thought of facing Borkas and Farrel here made fresh beads of sweat break out on his forehead.

'Hello. Were you looking for me?'

The voice did not belong to either of the boys. It was female, rich, melodious and strangely familiar, but he had no conscious memory of having heard it before. No woman in his village spoke with such regal tones, yet he had met none from outside that circle.

'It's good to see you're not afraid of heights. The Oracle is calling. Your time is here.'

Being careful to place his feet securely, Elian

4

turned slowly to face the owner of the enigmatic voice. He raised his eyes and his mouth formed a large O as he struggled to take in what he saw.

A dragon was standing on the base of the Finger with its wings partially furled: a huge, glorious dragon with glowing golden scales and bright horns. A crest, strengthened with ridges, ran down the middle of her back to a long tail and her great talons gleamed as if polished. Elian looked into her mesmerising eyes and for a moment he was lost. They were great windows of amber, opening into an abyss of immeasurable depth.

A waft of dry, musky scent invaded his nostrils as his air-starved lungs forced him to resume breathing. It reminded him of summer fields with just a hint of something tantalisingly exotic that again was familiar, yet unidentifiable.

With a determined effort, he wrenched his gaze from the dragon's eyes, but his focus did not shift far. There was one area of the dragon that inevitably drew his attention – the rows of long, pointed teeth.

Panic surged within him. The dragon had no rider. It was dangerous. It had to be. He looked around wildly, as if expecting to find some miraculous escape route. There was none. He was trapped.

The dragon took a step forwards.

Elian instinctively took two steps backwards and

lifted his hands, as if to push the dragon away. 'Don't come any closer!' he said, his voice sounding ragged even in his own ears.

'*Come to me. I've waited a long time for this moment. Your destiny is upon you.*'

It suddenly occurred to Elian that the dragon was communicating directly with his mind, but what it – she – was saying made no sense. Destiny? What destiny? Was this a trick used by dragons to gain easy meat? Was this what the village teacher had meant by the 'special powers' of dragons?

Without thinking, he took another step backwards. A fragment of rock crumbled and his right foot twisted. A startled shock wave of panic surged through him as he windmilled his arms in an effort to regain his balance. He failed. His centre of gravity had shifted too far to the right. The moment of realisation as he toppled felt lazy and detached. As he passed the point of no return his mind suddenly flashed through layers of panic to a new level of consciousness.

'*Fool!*' he heard the dragon exclaim in his mind. A yell formed in his throat, triggered more by the dragon's sudden surge towards him than any anticipation of the long fall. Her jaws opened wide as she lunged. She missed – barely – but during his first tumbling revolution, Elian realised she had not given up on her prey. The dragon had dived off the cliff and was also in freefall, arrowing down in pursuit.

Even though he was yelling uncontrollably, inside, Elian felt strangely calm. He was going to die – that was accepted. What was more difficult to decide was if his fall had lengthened his life, or shortened it. How long could he have kept the dragon talking before it killed him? He knew he had a slow count of approximately twenty-one (if his experiments with stones were representative) of life remaining. His yell petered out as his lungs emptied, but his thoughts raced on as he plummeted towards the valley below.

Air dragged at his clothing and roared in his ears. His fair hair, normally clean and neatly brushed at the insistence of his mother, felt as though it was being pulled from its roots. And his vision was blurred – not by tears, for no tears could form without being blasted away – but by his eyes drying and distorting in the pummelling airflow. What was more, he was still accelerating. He could feel it.

Turning face down, his cheeks billowed and flapped in a most insane manner. He could stop them by clenching his mouth shut and tightening his cheek muscles, but in a crazy sort of way it felt good to relax and experience a few new things.

Would he have time to register pain before he died? No. When he hit the ground, it would end in an instant. Another revolution and it felt as though the air had lifted the eyelids from his eyes. The pressure in his ears was building painfully and occasional flashes of blurred vision revealed the dragon catching up fast. Would he be allowed to meet his end on the rocks, or would he be torn apart by the dragon first?

'*Got you!*'

The female voice in his mind again. So he, Elian, son of Raim, was to be dragon food. But how many others from the village would have such a spectacular death? he rationalised.

A fearful, wrenching force squeezed and twisted his body as a double cage of talons snapped shut around him. The shock as the simultaneous slap of air met the dragon's unfurled wings felt like a crushing body punch. The impact spawned flashing stars of light that danced before his eyes as she deflected them out of the headlong dive.

Once in level flight, the pressure on Elian's chest, stomach and legs reduced until he felt as if he were simply laid across the talons like a sparsely slatted bed. With surprise he realised the grip of the dragon was most gentle.

He swallowed and his ears popped painfully.

Elian winced, but the pain receded quickly and his hearing was abruptly restored. The air-rush died down, and as his eyes rediscovered their focus, he found he was face down, gliding noiselessly southwards across the treetops in the Haleen Valley basin. It was the most exhilarating feeling he had ever experienced. For a moment he felt like hooting for joy, but then the thought of his imminent fate reasserted its hold.

In his mind he heard the dragon chuckle.

It's not fair, he decided. It's bad enough that I'm going to be a dragon's lunch, but listening to her amused anticipation of eating me makes it so much worse.

A clearing in the trees opened up ahead of them.

'Prepare yourself. We're going to land.'

They swooped down into the clearing until Elian was all but being brushed against the long grass. Then, in an instant, the dragon back-winged almost to a hover and dropped him. He fell no more than the length of a forearm into long, soft grass, his forward momentum so small that he only rolled over twice before coming to rest on his back. In dazed amazement he stared up at the sky.

For several heartbeats he remained still, his body tense, waiting for the dragon's head to descend, its jaws gaping. When after a short time nothing had happened, Elian eased himself up on his elbows to see over the top of the grass. The dragon was curled nearby with her long, wedge-shaped head angled in his direction and her huge, amazing eyes watching his every movement.

Something inside Elian snapped. 'What do you want?' he yelled suddenly, forcing himself to his feet. 'Am I supposed to run now? Can't you just eat me and be done with it?'

The enormous head rose slightly and the eyes fixed on him. If Elian had not known better, he would have thought the dragon was looking at him with mild disapproval.

'*I'd really rather you didn't run,*' she replied in his mind, '*for then I'd be forced to come after you. Perhaps it would help if we were properly introduced. Elian, I am Aurora . . . your dragon.*'

Chapter Two
Dragonriders

'What's wrong, Nolita? You look like you're expecting to see a ghost behind every tree.'

'I . . . I'm not sure, Sable,' Nolita replied, her eyes constantly on the move and her body taut. 'It's just a feeling, but it's growing stronger. It's as if someone's watching me. I . . . it's . . . well, it's not nice.'

Sable looked around. The tree trunks were well spaced here, so she could see a fair distance either side of the path. Nothing moved. It looked as if her younger sister's imagination were getting the better of her. Sable gave Nolita a comforting smile and caught hold of her hand to give it a squeeze.

'It's all right,' she said, looking straight into Nolita's darting blue eyes. 'It's probably just Balard messing around. He's taken a mischievous turn recently. I'll have words with him later. If necessary I'll get Father to talk to him.'

'It's not Balard,' Nolita replied instantly. 'I . . .' Nolita shook herself and gave a nervous giggle. 'Oh, I'm probably getting all upset over nothing. If it *is* Balard, or one of the village boys playing games, then they'll regret it,' she added, deliberately projecting her voice to make sure it could be heard some distance away.

'That's for sure!' Sable agreed. Nolita had her problems, but she could hold her own. She may have only seen thirteen summers, but few of her peers would face her with confidence when she was angry.

Nolita had always been able to cope with rats, spiders and snakes, which sent most girls, and a lot of the boys, running. But try to take her near a cow or a horse and she became a quivering wreck. She was similarly affected by heights and had never joined in with climbing games. Even watching others in the branches of trees was enough to set her shaking.

Until now her worst fears had been related only to heights or large animals. People, no matter how big, had never been a problem. Today marked a new and worrying development.

Sable turned back to the path, but kept hold of

her sister's hand. Nolita gave her fingers a grateful squeeze as they set off again. The neighbouring village was not much further. Mother had sent them to deliver a batch of herbs to the wise woman there. It was one of the few chores that no one minded, for the wise woman was well known for her cooking and her generosity. Those who visited her on errands often left with delicious cakes and sweetmeats to eat on the way home. Sable's stomach was grumbling at the thought.

'Look!' Sable exclaimed. 'There's the edge of the wood up ahead. Come on. You'll feel better once we're clear of the trees.'

A sudden rush of wind through the treetops above them caused both girls to look up. The air had been still and the thick canopy of leaves silent, until now. Was the weather on the turn? The surge of wind through the upper branches died as quickly as it began. Nolita tightened her fingers around her sister's, drawing comfort from the contact. It was eerie. A simultaneous gust of dread had swept through her as the rustling wave passed overhead.

'You're right, Sable. Let's run to the village. I feel so tight I might snap.'

The two girls sprang forwards, still holding hands. The first few strides were awkward, but they quickly matched their running rhythm, until each could feel the beat of the other's footfalls. It was less than two hundred paces to the edge of the wood, so they dashed through the trees at high speed. The release of energy felt good and Nolita's tension was just beginning to ease as they burst from beneath the trees into the open sunshine. Once clear of the wood, however, they skidded to an abrupt halt.

'Gods alive!' breathed Sable, totally awestruck.

Nolita made a noise like the yelp of a small dog whose tail had just been trodden on. She paused for the briefest of moments, and then she sprinted back into the trees faster than she had ever run before. Sable glanced after her sister, but was too filled with wonder to follow. It was as if she were under a spell. She rubbed at her eyes to make sure what she was seeing was real. It was. There, directly between her and the nearby village, was the most magnificent creature she had ever seen – a day dragon with gleaming blue scales and horns of creamy white. And he was looking right at her.

A continent away, Elian was similarly awestruck.

'I am Aurora, your dragon,' the dragon repeated after a short pause. 'But you may call me Ra, if you wish.' She chuckled. 'Ra! I've so looked forward to being called Ra. There was a place I once visited where

Ra was worshipped as the god of the sun. It's a good name.'

'"Your dragon"?' Elian asked, his mind struggling with the idea. 'What exactly do you mean by "your dragon"? And how do you know my name?'

'It is quite simple, Elian. I am a dragon. You are my dragonrider. I am your dragon. I waited a long time for you to be born and grow up. Now you are old enough, we have much to do together, you and I. As for your name, I heard it in your mind as you fell.'

Elian's jaw dropped slightly as his mind echoed with the dragon's words. 'You are my dragonrider . . .' You are my dragonrider? How could he be a dragonrider? He had never even met a dragon before!

'Me? A dragonrider?' he squeaked eventually. 'Why me?'

'Ah, the "why me" question! I was warned about those. Listen, Elian, there are no definitive answers to some questions. As far as dragons are concerned, humans are good for only two things. The first is to be dragonriders. The second is to be lunch – preferably lightly toasted.'

Elian gulped and Aurora's laughter sounded clearly in his mind.

'Sorry! Excuse my little joke, but after all your recent thoughts about being eaten it was hard to resist. Humans don't actually have much flavour. They're all right as a last resort, but a nice plump deer is much tastier. Suffice it to say that a dragon always knows her rider. It's instinctive. I knew the moment you were birthed, Elian. I waited centuries for that instant. As soon as I felt it, I knew my time was approaching. It was hard to wait these last few years for you to grow to transition. Every dragon has but one rider, Elian. You are mine. I am yours. We are destined to be together. Can you deny the bond? Did you not recognise my voice?'

It sounded so simple, yet also beyond comprehension. Elian was not ready to answer the dragon's questions yet, so he avoided them by asking more of his own.

'Centuries? Just how old are you? And, I hear you in my head, but you understand me if I speak aloud. I don't understand. How does that work?'

'Did no one ever tell you that it's rude to ask a lady her age?' Aurora answered, giving a little snort of disapproval. 'I know your mind is brimming with questions and I'm sure we'll get around to them all eventually. As for how I understand your strange speech – that's easy. The noises you make with your mouth are mirrored in your mind with images and words. It is unnecessary to speak aloud, but if you're more comfortable with this, I understand. It takes practice to discipline your thoughts.'

'So do dragons speak to one another in the same way? Or do you sort of look into one another's minds and take the information you need?' Elian asked, fascinated by the concept.

'We speak to one another by projecting thoughts, as I am speaking to you now,' she replied. 'We cannot read one another's minds as you read a book – well, we can, but only under very special circumstances. Our thoughts remain private unless we actively make them public. A dragon with a strong mind can overcome another and search through his thoughts at will, but to do so is forbidden under dragon law. Likewise, a dragon can overcome a human mind by force, but that is also forbidden. Reading surface thoughts, or the thoughts of a dragon who chooses to open their mind, is different. Similarly, our bond opens a channel that will develop until we each instinctively know what the other is thinking. Tell me, Elian, how much do you know about dragons?'

It was a good question. One that left Elian pondering on what little he knew.

'That's hard to say, exactly,' he answered slowly. 'The village teacher said to meet a dragon without a rider was to face a danger without parallel.'

'That isn't a bad philosophy to adopt, but it's not entirely accurate. Rogue dragons are dangerous, it's true, but rogue dragons are rare.'

17

'So what's a rogue dragon, if it isn't one without a rider?' Elian asked.

'*A rogue dragon is one who has lost its rider before completing their life's purpose – the reason for the dragon's existence. This constitutes such a dramatic failure that it can sometimes drive the dragon insane with grief. This life purpose is what all real dragons live for. Rogues are very rare, but I will not deny their existence.*'

'Life purpose? *Real* dragons?' Elian asked, his confusion mounting. 'Now you've completely lost me.'

'*There are four types of real dragons,*' Aurora explained patiently. '*I discount the ice dragons of the far south and the water dragons that inhabit the deeps of the oceans, for they live according to their own purposes. We do not mix with such types. The real dragons are the dragons of the day, with their scales of cornflower blue, nobler than the greatest of knights, and with hearts filled with the utmost bravery. Then there are the dark dragons of the night: black as coal with eyes of burning orange, filled with dread anger . . .*'

'Yes, I've heard of them,' Elian admitted, his voice meek and awed by the intensity of feeling he was sensing along with Aurora's words.

'*And, of course, there are the dusk dragons: rare as*

sapphires, dusty blue-grey with proud eyes of silver, enigmatic and full of ancient wisdom.'

'None of those descriptions fit you, Ra. I've heard tales of day dragons and dark rumours of night dragons, but dusk dragons? Are they half-breeds? The result of a mating between a day and a night dragon?'

'No! Nothing like that! It has to do with the time when the dragon hatches. Fear not, Elian. All will become clear. You are right — none of those descriptions fit me, for I am a dragon most rare. I, Elian, am a dawn dragon. This means nothing to you, for you are in ignorance of what it means to be a dragonrider at all, much less the rider of a dawn dragon. Come. Take up your destiny. Climb on my back and I shall show you what it means to be a dragonrider.'

The thought of powering up into the sky on the back of a dragon was both exciting and terrifying — the idea that this dragon was his life partner, even more so. Should he do it? Was this really happening? His voice cracked as he stammered his reply.

'How do I climb up?'

'Here, use my foreleg,' Aurora offered, extending her left foreleg towards Elian.

'This is really happening, isn't it? I'm not dreaming?'

'No, you are not dreaming,' the dragon replied, her

aloof amusement filling his mind. 'Come, Elian, we have a great deal to do. You humans don't live very long. Seize the moment. Ride, and we shall meet our destiny together.'

Elian walked tentatively forwards and placed his hand on Aurora's foreleg, watching intently for any sign of deception. What am I thinking of? he mused wryly. If she wanted to kill me, I would be dead by now. His belly felt as if it were full of leaping frogs and his mouth was suddenly as dry as it had been during his fall. The great amber eyes of the dragon watched him impassively.

Whatever texture Elian had been expecting of a dragon's scales, the sensation that met his fingertips was not it. Aurora's golden-orange scales gleamed, almost as if they were lit from within. Their shine gave the impression of hardness, yet they were strangely soft to the touch. They looked like armour, but felt as if they offered little more protection than human skin.

'They are tougher than they feel. Don't worry, Elian, you won't hurt me. Come on. Climb up.'

It felt strange beyond anything that Elian had ever imagined, but he half crawled, half scrabbled his way up Aurora's leg to her shoulder. As the dragon made no move to stop him, the reality of his situation began to sink in. Unbelievable as it seemed, the dragon's voice inside his head was real – and he was about to ride her.

'*That's it. Now sit yourself between two of my ridges. No, not there. Go back two more ridges . . . that's it. The balance there will be better for both of us. Are you ready?*'

'What a question!' Elian laughed. 'If I'd prepared all my life, I wouldn't be ready for this. I'm sitting on a dragon's back. Am I sane? I've no idea what's happening, but I don't care. It feels great! I'm as ready now as I'll ever be.'

'*Good. Hold on tight. I'm going to take you for a little ride.*'

Elian gripped the ridge in front of him as tightly as he could.

Aurora turned her body until she was facing southwards along the length of the clearing. Elian felt the bunching of her muscles beneath him and he braced himself, leaning forwards until his cheek was alongside the ridge that he was gripping. At the same time, he clamped his legs as tight as he could to the dragon's body, though it was not easy. The dragon's back was far wider than that of his pony and the muscles along his inner thighs protested at the stretching.

'AAAARRR . . .!'

The cry broke from Elian's throat as Aurora

exploded forwards at a speed far greater than the fastest horse Elian had ever ridden. Great leathery wings suddenly swept out, forwards and down, taking a massive bite at the air. The whoosh of Ra's first flapping motion was huge and Elian felt the dragon's feet skip off the ground. Air rushed past as the dragon continued to accelerate. Elian's stomach threatened to lurch up into his throat as she dipped back to the ground and her great wings circled back for another sweep.

'. . . RRRRGGGGHHHH!'

Elian's cry petered out. He sucked in another breath.

'*Here we go,*' Aurora's voice warned, and she swept forwards and down even harder with her wings. The ground fell away beneath them and Elian continued to yell uncontrollably. The rushing wind made his eyes water. Everything was blurred, but he knew he was now airborne and climbing.

'*Would you mind keeping down the noise back there? It's very distracting, you know. I wouldn't want to crash into anything.*'

Elian suspected that Aurora was joking again, but he was not about to take any chances. With her regal tones and imperious manner, she was more than a little scary. Chastened, he clamped his jaw shut and concentrated on blinking as fast as he

WITHDRAWN FROM CIRCULATION

could. He doubted he could have prised his fingers from their death grip on Ra's back ridge to wipe away his tears even if he had dared. He had no idea how high he was, but he did not think a fall would be a good idea.

'No,' Ra said, still listening to his thoughts. '*It wouldn't be a good idea. We're too high for you to survive a fall, but not yet high enough to give me much chance of catching you. If you feel you're slipping, then let me know. I'll do my best to help you regain your balance. I haven't waited all this time just to let you fall and die before we've got to know one another properly.*'

It took a moment or two longer for Elian to clear his eyes of tears sufficiently to be able to see again. The rise and fall of Aurora's back with every wing-stroke settled into a regular rhythm, to which his body automatically adapted.

When Elian's vision finally cleared, he gasped. They were far above the highest treetops and still climbing. They were also covering ground at a tremendous rate.

The sensation was amazing. It was unlike anything Elian had ever imagined. The rush of wind, the great whooshing of Aurora's wingbeats and the unique view from her back gave him a feeling of detachment. The ground felt too far away to give a sense of height, even though they were not yet as high up as the Devil's Finger. The difference was hard to explain. It was as if the view across the landscape had lost all sense of reality. Flying on Aurora's back gave the distance to the ground a feeling of depth, rather than height, as if he was looking over the side of a boat into crystal clear water and seeing the bottom many spans below.

'*Fun, isn't it?*' Ra said.

'It's incredible! Totally fantastic!' Elian shouted back.

Elation took over. 'WAHOOO!' he yelled, raising his head in exultation. 'WAHOOO!' He started to laugh uncontrollably, his sheer joy over-whelming him, spilling out and leaving him gasping for breath again.

'*I'm glad you're enjoying it, dragonrider, for I sense we have a lot of flying ahead of us.*'

'Where are we going, then?' Elian asked, his laughter dying away as the implications of that statement sank in.

'*Now?*' Ra asked.

'Yes.'

'*Well, to begin with, I think I had better take you home. You'll need provisions, clothes and travel gear. I'm sure you'll also want to say goodbye to your family. You probably won't see them again for some time. Our path together is beckoning. There's no time for me to* teach you the finer points of flying. You will have to learn as you go. My senses tell me we need to visit the Oracle soon. Time waits for neither man nor dragon.'

Elian wanted to ask Ra what she meant by 'the Oracle'. But first, he had a more important request. 'If you're taking me home, can we make a little side stop first?'

'That depends,' Ra answered, caution reflected in her tone. 'What have you got in mind?'

'I've an old score to settle with a couple of boys who'd really benefit from meeting a dragon.'

Chapter Three
Hunter and Hunted

'*If you wish to gain revenge upon these boys, Elian, I should warn you that I am no weapon to be used at your bidding.*' The full weight of Aurora's most imperious tones brooked no argument.

'No! Of course not, Ra! I don't want you to *hurt* them — but I hoped you might agree to give them a bit of a fright. You see, Borkas and Farrel have made life a misery for my friends and me. They're the worst sorts of bullies — mean-spirited and cruel. I just thought it would be great to give them a taste of what it feels like to be small and vulnerable, that's all.'

Aurora fell silent while she considered his request. Time stretched and Elian hardly dared to breathe.

'*Very well,*' she said eventually. '*Where will we find these boys?*'

'I expect they're waiting for me near the edge of the woods, not far from where we met,' Elian replied, unable to hide his excitement.

'*Then that's where we'll look.*'

Aurora suddenly dipped her left wing to turn and Elian grunted with surprise. An invisible force pressed him hard against Ra's back. He looked left and his stomach knotted with fear. The ground filled his view, yet despite the impossible angle he did not fall. He did not understand why, but he was very glad to be squashed firmly in place upon the dragon's back by what felt like a great, unseen hand.

'*Go with the turn, Elian. If you try to lean the other way, then you might fall off my other side when I roll out of it.*'

Elian wasn't about to argue. It felt wrong, but he did as he was told. Instinct and fear tightened his fingers until he was sure they would have to be prised free from Ra's neck ridge when he landed. Despite obediently leaning into the turn, he began to slide off her other side as she returned to level flight. Elian righted himself quickly, most grateful for the forewarning. It would take a while to get used to turns, he realised.

Aurora continued to power upwards, gaining altitude with every stroke of her wings. Elian glanced down and realised they were now heading back northwards along the line of the valley. It was not long before he could see the Devil's Finger, looking more impossible and sinister than ever from this angle. And he had walked nearly to the end! What had he been thinking of?

Before long they were level with the Finger and then above it, climbing further until they skimmed in and out of the base of the cloud layer. Thin wisps wrapped around them in wraith-like tendrils, parting in swirls as they powered through.

'I'm going to climb through this. It's very thin, but you might get a bit wet.'

Elian did not answer. He was fascinated by the possibility of being above the clouds. He had once looked down into the Haleen Valley when there had been fog in the valley basin. The view then had been spectacular, but to be above the clouds – what would that be like?

A few more powerful down-strokes of Ra's wings and they plunged into a waking nightmare of whiteness. The temperature dropped and Elian shivered. Flying blind into what felt like driving fog was terrifying. Squinting into the damp, milky mist, all he could see was Ra's back and wings. It was as if they had entered a void. Could Aurora see where she was going? Although Elian knew they were above the edge of the Great Escarpment, it was easy to imagine flying blind into a cliff.

Within a few heartbeats he was soaked. Tiny droplets of water beaded on his skin, collecting together and growing before running in rivulets, driven by the airflow. The wet, white terror was brief. They punched out of the top of the cloud into brilliant sunshine and Elian found he was still squinting, but this time against the light. The sky above was a stunning blue and the top surface of the cloud was a dazzling white. Although he was shivering with cold, he felt a warm flood of elation course through him. It was as if they were flying above a sea of the most perfectly mashed potato – fluffy and white, with not even the slightest hint of unpeeled skin to mar its purity.

As they climbed still higher, Elian realised the white carpet was not complete. Small breaks were appearing in the cloud, but it would be some time before the sun was strong enough to break it up more thoroughly.

'How can you tell where we are?' Elian shouted.

'*To be honest, I can't tell exactly,*' Ra responded. '*However, I can estimate very well. Also, if I concentrate, I can sense the presence of humans. There are two of your kind below us.*'

'Can you hear their thoughts?'

'I can hear echoes of their surface thoughts, but cannot read them with absolute clarity. From what I sense of these two, they're up to no good.'

'That'll be Borkas and Farrel!' he said excitedly. 'Can you land us somewhere close, but where they won't see us come down? I've got an idea.'

Ra turned gently to the right and entered a shallow, descending spiral that took them back into the cloud. Remaining close to the base of the cloud, so that she could see the ground directly below, she cruised to find a suitable place to land. It did not take long. She picked her point and dropped steeply, before pitching neatly out of the dive and killing her forward motion with a clever twist of her wings. They landed with the lightest of touches.

Elian eased his right leg over to join his left and slid to the ground, where he collapsed in a heap, clutching at his groin in pain.

'What's the matter, Elian? Are you all right?'

'Yes ... and no,' he groaned. 'It's just that riding you isn't like riding a horse. My legs don't feel as if they were meant to split that wide. I've over-stretched some muscles in a rather delicate place.'

Aurora gave a little snort and Elian sensed her amusement. 'You'll get used to it quickly enough, dragonrider, though a dragon saddle would help. Now, what is your plan?'

Elian outlined what he had in mind and she snorted again.

'*Crude, but effective,*' she acceded. '*Very well. I shall be listening to your thoughts. I'll play my part, do not fear.*'

With that she turned and launched across the heath, away from where the two boys were waiting. Elian caught up with her climb quickly and watched the cloud swallow her without so much as a swirl to mark her passage. With another groan and a lot of wincing, he got to his feet and began moving gingerly forwards.

The worst of the pain in his groin had gone by the time Elian caught up with the two bullies. They had given up on him and were walking back towards the village. It took a while for the boys to notice Elian. When they did, however, they turned instantly to meet him, chatting to one another and grinning with wicked anticipation. He allowed himself a quiet smile of his own.

'What d'you think *you* have to smile about, Elian?' Borkas sneered.

'I'm enjoying the moment, Borkas,' he replied calmly, maintaining his smile. 'Because this is the last time you'll ever try to bully anyone from our village.'

The two large lads stopped five paces short of

him. They looked firstly at one another, then all around them, and finally back at Elian.

'And what makes you think you can stop us, dungball?' Farrel scoffed.

'I've got a new friend who's looking out for me. She's decided it's time you changed your ways. In fact she's promised that if you don't, she'll have you for breakfast.'

The two boys exploded into gales of laughter. 'A girl!' Borkas roared. 'He thinks hiding behind the skirts of a girl is going to stop us!'

'What a turkey!' agreed Farrel. 'Come on. Let's give him a little reminder of how it works before his girlfriend turns up to scare us.'

'Oh, it's far too late for that,' Elian said, standing his ground as the two boys curled their fingers into fists and took the first step towards him.

A sudden gust of wind from behind them was followed by a loud thud and a long, deep, shuddering snort. Borkas and Farrel froze. With painful slowness, they turned inwards towards one another and onwards until they came face to face with Aurora, whose nostrils were less than a handspan behind them.

'*Block your ears, Elian,*' she warned.

He did so instantly, watching with amused fascination as she inhaled a huge breath, drawing her head up and away from the two terrified boys. With startling speed, she lunged towards them. Her jaws opened wide and she let loose a deafening roar that literally blew the hair on the boys' heads straight out behind them. Borkas and Farrel were suddenly faced with a very close up view of her most impressive rows of large, razor-sharp teeth, her long, pointed tongue and her deep, deep gullet.

The roar ended. The two bullies remained motionless for a single heartbeat, staring in total shock into the huge dragon eyes regarding them from just beyond her teeth. Then they turned and ran like Elian had never seen them run before. And as they ran, they screamed in abject terror.

Elian removed his fingers from his ears. His lips formed a broad grin of satisfaction as he watched them go.

'*Do you think that will do it?*'

'Oh yes, Ra!' he chuckled. 'That was as good as it gets! Borkas and Farrel nearly wet themselves! After that I'd be surprised if they ever bullied anyone again.'

'He gives me the creeps, Tembo. I don't know if it's his eyes or his uncanny ability to read signs that no one else can see, but there's something unnatural about him.'

Tembo shrugged his great shoulders. 'You should be grateful, Husam. He's the best dragon tracker around. Without him we'd all be forced to work hard for a living. He's a bit strange, but his senses make up for it. Look. He's found something.'

Husam looked up at his hulking friend: loyal, trusting and immensely strong, Tembo was the best sort of person to have as a hunting partner. He appeared every inch the gentle giant, but was surprisingly fast and deadly with a spear. His face looked as if a child had modelled it from clay, squashing a sausage-shaped nose onto the middle and giving him oversized ears that stuck out from the sides of his head like flaps. His features made him look simple and his manner did little to dispel that impression. However, underneath the comic features was a many-faceted character, who could solve even the most difficult of puzzles.

They had worked together for two years before joining Kasau's party. As a team they had done well, but they had never known success on the scale they had enjoyed since joining the quiet hunter. Kasau had instincts unlike anybody else. He did not need to hear rumour of rogue dragons terrorising villages. It was almost as if he knew where they would be before the dragons did. He did not talk much, but when he did, everyone listened.

Tembo was right. Kasau had found something. Husam watched the hunter stalk across to the nearby stand of trees and back again. The hairs on the back of Husam's neck prickled, as they often did when watching Kasau at work. Damn but the man is spooky, he thought as Kasau straightened and walked back towards the rest of the party. Even from some distance away, Husam could see his eyes. It was hard to ignore them. They were both brown, but where the left was a dark, chocolate colour, the right was almost orange. Mismatched eyes were said to be a sign of the devil. Husam had not yet seen any evidence of evil, but he felt something – an awkward sense of discomfort in Kasau's presence that he could not shake.

'She is close,' Kasau reported in his soft voice. 'If this hunt is successful, we will all be rich. I can now confirm she's a dawn dragon.'

'A dawn dragon! That's fantastic, Kasau!'

'She's close, you say? In which direction?'

'How big is she?'

The questions arrowed in thick and fast. Husam noted that Kasau did not respond to any of them. Instead the dragonhunter held up a hand for silence.

'There's a problem,' he said, his voice flat and

cold. His eyes moved from one member of the party to another, settling briefly on each and then moving on. When his eyes met Husam's, his pause was a little longer. A shiver ran down Husam's spine. For a moment he felt as if the strange hunter were looking into his soul. 'The dragon has met her rider,' Kasau finished.

Groans rippled through the party.

Rogue dragons were the justification for dragon hunting. Killing those insane dragons was seen as a mercy to the dragon and a necessity to the communities the dragons terrorised. If dragonhunters sometimes killed riderless dragons that were not true rogues, then the authorities tended to turn a blind eye – especially as the carcasses had properties that were beneficial to the human communities. However, to kill a dragon that had a dragonrider was a serious offence. Aside from the penalties the authorities placed on such an act, there was also the danger that other members of the dragonrider community might seek revenge. Dragonhunters who flouted this law did not have a great life expectancy.

Kasau again raised his hand for silence.

'Who here wants to get rich?' he asked. His voice was soft, but the words carried a weight that lent its own volume.

Is this the evil I feared? thought Husam, his heart racing. Could Kasau be an agent of the devil?

'We can't risk killing a dragon that has a rider,' he said aloud in a firm voice. 'It's wrong. Besides, we'd not live to enjoy the rewards.'

Where had that last sentence come from? Kasau stared at him unblinking. Try as he might, Husam could not break eye contact. It was as if Kasau was holding his head in an invisible vice. Had the quiet hunter somehow transferred that thought into his brain?

'Who would know?' Kasau asked, continuing to hold Husam with his gaze. The dragonhunter's soft voice seemed to echo inside Husam's head. It was a strange sensation. 'Listen – the dragon has just met her rider for the first time. The dragonrider community are not yet aware of their partnership. Until the dragon takes her rider to her dragon enclave, we can continue to hunt her without worrying about other dragons or riders.'

'But what about the rider?' Husam asked pointedly. 'Are you suggesting we should kill him too?'

'It might be kind to do so, but it won't be necessary,' Kasau replied, his soft voice cold and clinical. 'Upon the death of his dragon, the rider will lose his mind. No one takes the word of a jabbering lunatic seriously.'

A wave of muttering swept through the party. Kasau broke eye contact with Husam and looked around the group. Husam felt suddenly groggy. He staggered slightly, but Tembo's arm was quick to steady him. He rubbed his eyes and pain started to pound in his forehead with the steady rhythm of a drumbeat.

He looked around to see how the rest of the party was receiving Kasau's suggestion. He could see that the quiet hunter was likely to split their group. Heated debate gripped them. It was a larger hunting party than was typical: nineteen strong, including Kasau. Even so, they had prospered under his leadership.

Maybe a split is what he intends, Husam mused, noting the gradual increase in volume of the muttering, as tones turned angry. Maybe he feels the group has grown too big. If the group does split, I could try for leadership of the second party. A leader's share of the spoils is always greater. This is not the only dragon. There will be other hunts.

A third time Kasau raised his hand for silence. It took a little longer this time, but gradually the muttering subsided.

'The tracks show the dragon is a mature, female dawn dragon. She is at the height of her powers. This is a dragon the like of which you will probably never see again in your lifetime. I'm not giving up the hunt. Now she has joined with her rider, she will fly to see the Dragon Spirit in Orupee. Anticipating her track is straightforward. We can set a trap for her. The Overlords will never know. Who amongst you will follow me?'

Some called *Aye* instantly. Others followed more reluctantly in dribs and drabs. Eventually the only two who had not responded were Tembo and Husam. Husam looked up at his friend. The big man looked back, his expression clear – whatever Husam did, Tembo would follow.

For a moment Husam was tempted to turn and walk away. This was wrong. He felt it in every fibre of his being, yet he could also feel the draw of the gold. A dawn dragon's bones, scales, hide, eyes and horns would be worth a fortune. Assuming they were successful, even with such a big party every one of them could retire a rich man.

'Aye,' he said through gritted teeth. 'And may the Creator have mercy on our souls.'

Chapter Four
Saying Farewell

Aurora landed in the fallow field next to the cottage where Elian and his parents lived. It was well that he lived on the edge of the village, for Ra would have had problems negotiating the narrow lanes without causing unwelcome damage to property.

'I think you had better get down quickly and talk with your people,' she suggested, watching with a wary eye towards the edge of the village. *'Some of them look as though they might have the wrong idea.'*

She was right. Despite the silent, gliding approach, their arrival had not gone unnoticed. A crowd of villagers was already congregating, with more running to join them by the heartbeat. The women gathered excited children close about their legs and some of the men were armed with crude weapons. As if they would be of any use against Ra, Elian thought, dismayed that anyone would consider harming his dragon.

Easing his right leg gingerly between Ra's ridges, he slid down her side with care to avoid a repeat of his embarrassing collapse earlier. He walked forwards, gritting his teeth against the renewed pain in his upper legs and groin.

'It's all right, everyone. You can relax,' he called out, raising his hands in a calming gesture. Aurora lowered her head until her bottom jaw rested on the ground next to him. He placed a hand on the side of her face and patted her gently. 'Let me introduce Aurora – my dragon.'

It was unfortunate that his mother, Megan, had just emerged from the front door as he bellowed out his news. Her eyes first went wide with shock, and then rolled up in her head. She collapsed with all the grace of a soggy lettuce.

'Mother!'

Elian raced across the field and vaulted over the low, stone wall that marked out the edge of the garden. His father appeared through the door even as Elian reached his mother's side.

'Megan? Megan!' Raim's voice was anxious as he knelt down at his wife's side and gently patted her face in an effort to bring her round. 'What happened, Elian? Did you see her fall?'

As Raim looked up at Elian, he became aware of the crowd of people gathered at the end of the garden.

'What are they all doing here?' he asked. 'Have you been causing trouble, young ...' Raim did not finish. Megan chose that moment to stir. Her eyes fluttered open and she smiled as she saw her husband and son looking down at her.

At that same moment a shadow fell over them. Megan's eyes went wide. She gave a piercing scream and passed out again. Raim looked round sharply. His eyes first focused on the huge body of the dragon only a few paces away. It took a moment for him to take in what he was looking at. Then slowly – painfully slowly – his head tipped further and further back as he followed the neck of the dragon up until his eyes met Aurora's and took in her toothy grin.

Ra had followed Elian silently until she was as close as she could get to the house without damaging the garden wall. Her head extended on her long neck well over the wall as she attempted to get a closer look at Elian's parents.

'Get into the house, Elian,' Raim ordered, his voice low, but firm. 'Don't make any sudden moves. Just ease inside the door and everything will be fine.'

'Of course everything will be fine, Father. This

is Aurora. She's my dragon. Well, she's not my dragon in the sense that I own her. It's a bit more complicated than that. We sort of own each other, really, but, well ... Ra, this is my father. Father, meet Ra.'

'I'm not going to tell you again, Elian. Inside the house – now!' Raim growled.

'Father, listen to me. I know this sounds unlikely, but I just found out that I'm a dragonrider. This is my dragon.' He looked up apologetically at Ra. 'I'm sorry about this. Would you mind backing away while I talk with my father, Aurora? It's bound to be a shock. No one from around here has become a dragonrider in a very long time.'

'*Certainly, Elian,*' Ra replied, bowing her head. '*Your parents seem good people. Your father is a brave man. He thought to protect you and your mother from me. It was a noble gesture. Please tell him I'm pleased to have gained a dragonrider born from such a fine family.*'

'I will. Thank you, Aurora,' Elian replied aloud for his father's benefit.

Raim looked in astonishment as the dragon's head turned away on her long neck and the huge beast walked off into the middle of the field where she curled up in a massive circle of scales, horns, ridges and teeth to wait. All eyes in the ever-growing crowd followed her every move.

'It can't be true,' Raim stammered after a long pause.

'It is, Father. I'm a dragonrider. Ra says what you just did was very brave and that she's pleased to see her rider has a courageous father.'

'But you're too young. You can't be a dragon-rider. You're too young.'

'I've seen fourteen summers, Father. I'm nearly a grown man.'

'But you're *not* a grown man, Elian. You're not old enough to be flying around on a dragon. Riding a dragon is terribly dangerous.'

'And you would know this because . . .'

'Don't be cheeky, Elian. You're not improving your position with your disrespect.' Megan stirred again. Raim's hands automatically began to stroke her cheek and comb her hair with his fingers. 'Go and fetch some water for your mother. No doubt she'll need something stronger when you tell your story later, but water would be good for now.' Raim looked up at the crowd, ogling from the bottom of his small garden. Virtually everyone in the village was there now. 'Please go home, every-one,' he said, projecting his voice without shouting. 'I'd like to talk to all the menfolk later at the meeting house, but for now, please leave us to our family business.'

An excited buzz of muttering swept through the previously silent crowd as they started to disperse to their houses. A small number of children remained to watch the dragon, but most were called away by concerned parents. Elian was suitably contrite when he returned with the water.

'The beast ... Is it gone? Was it real?' Megan muttered, as she began to surface again from her fainting spell.

'Hush now, Megan. Everything is fine. Here – sip this water. It'll help. That's right. Now, let's get you inside and I'll have Elian fetch you a nice hot cup of spiced wine. You'll feel much better with a warm drink inside you.'

'Yes. Yes, that would be nice. I had the most horrible waking dream, Raim. I could have sworn I saw a dragon.'

'You—' Elian began.

'Elian! Help me lift your mother inside, would you?' Raim barked. His interruption was sharp, but his voice was not unkind. 'Careful now! I think she might have some bruising from her fall.'

Elian bit his lip as he lent his strength to help lift his mother. She was not heavy, being of slight build and half a hand shorter than her son. Between them, they lifted her easily and carried her through to the small living area to the right of the front door. Once sitting in her favourite chair, Megan regained some of her normal colour.

'Heat some wine, would you please, Elian?' asked his father. 'Use the spices in the upper cupboard to flavour it; they're fresher. A sharp taste would be best. I'll have a cup too, as you're preparing it.'

'Yes, Father.'

Elian did as he was bid. He went to the kitchen, poured some wine from a skin into a small pot and hung it over the fire. He was careful to hang it on one of the higher hooks to avoid scorching the pan. The wine was best warm, rather than boiling. He had not tried to get anything down from the top cupboard for some months. To his surprise, the fresh spices were well within his reach. He added some of them to the pot and returned the rest to the cupboard.

The smell of the warming wine brought memories of good times. Spiced wine was a luxury saved for special occasions, such as midwinter feast days, summer festivals and naming days. These were good days, filled with laughter, smiles and fine food. This was a good day, too, but Elian doubted his parents were about to celebrate his change of status. The next few hours would be difficult.

'*It would be best to break the news to them quickly*

that you will be leaving, Elian. We cannot linger here for long.'

Aurora's voice in his mind felt more normal each time she spoke to him. What was most strange was the setting. The kitchen had been the centre of his life until now. True, he had a tiny cubicle of a room that was his private space, but life in the cottage revolved around the kitchen. There was always something to be done.

Life in a rural household on the high plain was simple. Food was life. Whether it was being prepared for eating, storage, or to use as barter for other necessities, it was always at the centre of the day's activities. What people did not grow, raise, catch, or hunt was bought by exchange at the local market, or from travelling tinkers. Nothing was wasted. Nothing was useless.

The kitchen was orderly and functional. Knives, spatulas, pots and spoons all had their own special place. Strings of onions and garlic bulbs hung from hooks, while rows of sealed pots and jars were neatly stacked on wall shelves and inside the large larder cupboard that was almost a room in its own right. Two small windows gave natural light to the room, but oil lamps were often lit on poor weather days.

'How do I tell them, Ra? It'll break my mother's heart,' he whispered.

'A wise old dragon once told me that to meet your destiny, you must first build a history. Destiny is calling us, Elian. We must leave to build our history together. Do not worry. Your father is no fool. He already knows you must go.'

'He does?'

'Of course!' Ra said, her voice firm with confidence. 'He knew the moment he saw me. There is no denying the bond between dragon and rider. Our meeting has been destined since the beginning of time. Nothing can prevent our partnership now. Your parents may not like your leaving, but neither will they try to stop you. Trust me, Elian. You must be open and honest. They will do their part.'

To Elian's surprise, Ra was right. By the time the wine had warmed sufficiently and he had carefully poured it into two cups, Raim had clearly had quiet words with his wife. Tears filled Megan's eyes as Elian entered the room.

'Go and get another cup, Elian. This is a moment for sharing.' Raim's tone was as serious as his face. He looked different – strangely old – as if the recognition of his son's future had placed a great weight on his shoulders. Elian felt emotion swell in his heart as he glimpsed a flash of what his parents must be feeling. Tears welled in his eyes as he poured the beaker of wine. He blinked them away.

It would not do to cry like a baby at such a time. If the other village boys found out ... but did it matter what the other boys thought? No. Such things would never be a consideration again. He was a dragonrider. As such, he held status above any of the other boys.

'*Good. You're beginning to understand.*'

Elian did not answer. He returned to the living area with his wine. The reality of his situation was finally sinking in. He had always loved his parents. To see them like this was heartbreaking. Emotions warred on their faces. Pride battled with worry. Fear for the future competed with joy at his good fortune. But clearly laced through every other emotion was love.

Raim raised his cup. 'To Elian – man, dragonrider and son. Wishing you happiness and long life. No matter where your path leads, never forget there is a place at the table here for you.'

They all drank. The tears in Raim's eyes made Elian more comfortable with those welling in his own. Megan wept in floods. Before he knew it, both parents had drawn him into a hug. It felt good. Safe. Homely. When they finally broke from it, Elian felt strangely empty, as if a part of his life were dying. Then, in a sudden emotional reversal, he felt the void fill and in that instant both he and Aurora felt the *click* of a perfect match as their souls met.

Although Ra did not say anything, Elian could feel the joy of her presence within him and he knew he would never be alone again. The feeling was not one of replacement, but of progression – almost like being reborn to begin a whole new life. His parents would always be special, but this new relationship was forged with an invisible connection more powerful than any ties of blood or friendship. It was a paradox, for though the link felt new, legends told that the connection between every dragon and rider had been written in the stars since the dawn of time. Something inside him felt the seed of truth in those old tales. The bond was predestined and special. There could be no regret.

Nolita had never known such fear. The beast was huge, and covered in scales and vicious horns. Although she knew it was a dragon, she could not bring herself to think of it by that name. It was a thing of nightmares – the very embodiment of her deepest, most secret terror, and it had haunted her for as long as she could remember.

She was back amongst the trees faster than she believed possible. The path was well worn and easy to follow. She flew along it, her feet hardly touching the ground. Her blond hair streamed out behind her like a three-dimensional golden flag, and as she ran, she screamed.

It took at least a minute for Nolita to notice that her throat hurt and her breathing was hampered by her screams. Regaining a small measure of control, she clamped her teeth together in a determined grimace and forced herself to focus on the path. Details of the beast had burned into her mind and haunted her as she ran. It was hard to concentrate, but she used her fear like a driving whip, urging speed, and reinforcing the need to put as much distance between her and it as possible.

It was about half a league to her home village. Although she and Sable had taken their time strolling through the woods, it did not take long for her to retrace her steps, running flat out the whole way. She raced to the centre of the small cluster of cottages and in through the door of her home.

'That was quick!' her mother said, looking up in surprise from the table where she was busy mending one of Balard's tunics. 'Did you race Sable back?'

'Sable!' Nolita exclaimed, panting heavily. 'I . . . I don't know what happened to her. There was a . . . I was scared. I . . . I ran. I'm so sorry.'

Tears streamed down Nolita's face. Her body was shaking uncontrollably and her eyes darted about with anxious anticipation. Emotions flashed and spun through her like a tornado. Horror and fear twisted into worry and self-loathing only to spin back to horror and fear. How could she have left her sister to face it alone? She should have at least urged Sable to follow. But she hadn't. Did that make her a bad person? Had it got Sable? Oh, gods! What if it had? How could she live with that?

'Calm down, Nolita. Take a deep breath. Now start again slowly. What happened? What scared you?'

'No! I must wash. I have to. Please, let me wash first.'

Her mother sighed. Nolita's obsession with washing her hands had become progressively worse over the last year. It appeared to be her instinctive response to a growing number of circumstances. Other little signs of ritualistic activities were creeping into her behaviour as well. It was worrying to see her daughter trapped in such a cycle, but she felt powerless to help break Nolita free of her obsession. She could not deny that the washing did help calm Nolita when she was stressed.

'Very well,' she agreed, 'but talk to me as you wash. If Sable's in trouble, we should send help immediately.'

'Y-yes, M-mother.'

Nolita grabbed one of the hand bowls, leaned out through the window and dipped it into the water butt outside, half filling it with water. She shook as she crossed to the table, spilling a trail of water across the floor, but she could not even think about pausing to mop it up. Her soap was in its usual place. As soon as she had it in her hands a calming sensation began to spread through her.

'It . . . it was horrible,' she began. 'Huge. Terrible. All horns and teeth and wings.'

'You met this thing?' her mother asked, her brows drawing into a frown. 'Where?'

'We had just reached the clearing on the other side of the woods. I think it must have flown over us as we were on our way. I felt it go by. I . . . I think . . .'

'What? What do you think, Nolita?'

'I think it was looking for me,' she said in a rush, tears dripping into the bowl.

'Hush now! That's nonsense and you know it. From what you've said, I would say you saw a dragon. Is that right?'

Nolita scrubbed furiously at her hands. She did not look up at her mother, but nodded quickly.

'Why on Areth would a dragon come looking for you, Nolita? That's just your fears speaking. Did you see the dragon's rider? He was probably visiting the village on a quest of some sort. Dragonriders do that, you know. Now try to calm down. Can you tell me what sort of dragon it was? What colour was it?'

'B-b-blue. It was b-blue. And I didn't see a rider.'

'A day dragon. That's good. The rider was probably in the village. Dragons are patient creatures, Nolita, and sensitive. The dragon was most likely waiting for its rider to complete his business. Well, I don't think Sable is in any danger, but I suppose I should ask one of the menfolk to go and take a look just in case.'

Just in case what, Nolita wondered. Just in case the beast was dangerous? Wasn't it a bit late for that? Why couldn't Mother see? The beast was hunting for her – Nolita – no one else. She had felt it. She had unconsciously known for years that it was coming. It had haunted her dreams and fed her fears with the promise that one day it would find her. Now it was here. Her nightmare had become a reality. She would have to leave to escape it. There was no time to lose. It would find her soon. She wasn't safe. She needed to go, and she needed to go now.

Nolita blinked away her tears. The washing had helped, but it was her decision to run away that gave her temporary control of her fear. She dried her hands and told her mother she would take the dirty water to the waste ditch.

Once outside the cottage she began to think through her plan. What did she need to take with her? She could not carry much. Any weight would slow her down. She would have to forage for food as she went. The question was: where should she go? Was there anywhere she *could* go to escape such a beast?

She tipped the dirty water into the waste ditch in a controlled stream. There was something hypnotising about the way the water splattered and gurgled in the mud. A shadow brushed her, moving at speed. She glanced up and her stomach instantly knotted with fear. It was too late to think about what to take. She was out of time. It was here. Without thinking, Nolita dropped the bowl and launched into a wild sprint for the nearby trees.

Chapter Five
Ambushed

If Elian was surprised by his parents' acceptance of his newfound status, he was stunned by the response of the rest of the village. That evening the men held a special raising ceremony for him, accepting him into the adult community. To his amazement and delight, his raising gift was a dragonrider's saddle. He had not known that such a thing existed within their small community. It transpired that by law, every tanner had to make and keep a dragon saddle against the day that a rider should need one. The tanner in his village had not neglected this duty and proudly presented it to the Cleric, who prayed a simple blessing over it before passing it to Elian.

The village elders had long ago decided that dragon lore would not be taught to youngsters. It was feared that knowledge of dragons would only encourage daydreaming amongst the young. However, it was a requirement of the adult community to know their duty to the fortunate few whom the dragons chose, so they were taught about dragons and dragonriders after their raising ceremony.

The problem with this system was obvious. Dragons sought out their riders as they reached puberty. If one were chosen from the village, the individual would know nothing of the history and place of dragonriders in society. This was the frustrating situation Elian faced. References made to him about his newfound role were more confusing than enlightening. Worse, he knew he would not be able to stay long enough to learn what he needed to know. He could feel Ra's need to leave, a need that could not be denied.

When the men had completed the special raising ceremony, the women of the village joined the celebration. They brought more surprise gifts, which Elian quickly realised would prove invaluable when he left to begin his new life.

First, a heavy, fur-lined sheepskin jacket, together with a matching pair of trousers. They were too big, but the women insisted he would grow into them soon enough. He was also given a leather, fur-lined hat, designed to cover the ears and secure under the chin; mitten gloves and a special pair of thick boots, again lined with fur. How they had such garments to give was again a source of mystery to him, for the weather in this part of Racafi rarely turned cold. 'How *is not important*,' Ra assured him. '*Take them and relay my thanks to your people, Elian, for the gifts are well given. You will be grateful for them soon enough.*'

The village blacksmith gave him his favourite gift of the evening: a sword. It was plain with a straight blade of medium length and weight, a leather-bound handle and a simple hand guard. It was presented in a scabbard that could either be attached to his waist belt, or strapped across his back. Elian accepted the gift gravely, though he was acutely aware of the frowns of disapproval and worry on his parents' faces. Would he have need of such a weapon? He hoped not. If he did, he would not know how to wield it. The gift raised the question in his mind once more: what exactly *was* his role as a dragonrider?

'*A question that begs much exploration, Elian. We can discuss your heritage at length when we are under-way. Enjoy the moment. Tomorrow we must leave. Our destiny calls.*'

Elian took Aurora's message to heart. He quickly realised that to be chosen as a dragonrider was a great honour, and that honour was reflected on the village. He managed to stop worrying and throw himself into the festivities, and the rest of the evening was a blur of music and dancing, laughter and tears.

The next morning, Elian's eyes burned from lack of sleep. The partying had continued well into the small hours of the morning – something he had never experienced before. All he wanted to do was to stay in bed, but he could feel Ra's desire to be under way. There was a sense of urgency in their bond that he could not ignore. He washed and dressed for what could be the last time in his home.

Nerves and excitement warred within him as he gathered his things. His stomach gnawed with hunger, or was it nervousness? He could not tell the difference.

'Good morning, Elian,' Raim said brightly as he walked through to the kitchen. 'Take a seat. Your mother has prepared a special farewell breakfast for you.'

The smell of the food tightened Elian's stomach even more. He had eaten so much the previous evening it seemed impossible that he could be hungry again already, but as he forked in the first mouthful, he realised he was. It would be a difficult balance, he realised, to eat enough to sate his hunger, but not so much that his nervousness might cause him embarrassment later. In his mind he sensed Ra's presence. She seemed mildly amused.

'*You won't think it funny if I vomit all over your back,*' he thought, directing a mental image of this to the corner of his mind where Aurora appeared to be.

'*If you do, then I'll have you polishing my scales all afternoon,*' she responded haughtily. '*That sort of behaviour is not acceptable for a dragonrider.*'

It took a great deal of self-control, but somehow Elian managed to do justice to the breakfast that Megan had prepared. She fussed around him, telling him how pale he looked, and asking him if he really felt up to leaving today. And where was he going, and how long would he be gone? In truth, he felt anything but ready, but Aurora was insistent.

'*We must go. We have to see the Oracle – the great Dragon Spirit who dwells in Orupee. My dragonsense tells me that any delay will be disastrous. As to how long we will be gone . . . I would not make any rash promises if I were you.*'

Still, it took until late morning for his mother to stop fussing. Her eyes were red and puffy.

'Don't worry, Mother. I'll be back. You'll see,' he called from Aurora's back. All right, Ra,' he added under his breath. 'Try to make it a smooth take-off, would you? I'm as jittery as a sheep that's caught sight of the shears. I don't want to embarrass myself in front of the entire village by falling off as we wave goodbye.'

Ra did not answer, but turned and launched across the field. With his gloved hands holding firmly onto the grips of the dragon saddle and his feet set in the stirrups, Elian felt in far less danger of falling off than he had when riding bareback. The saddle had taken a while to figure out, but once Elian had worked out how to fit it between Ra's ridges and where the straps went to secure it in place, he felt a lot more confident. The saddle also offered a degree of comfort that was most welcome.

With just a few powerful sweeps of Aurora's great wings, they were airborne and climbing.

'Hold on tight, Elian. We're going to give them a flypast to remember.'

'Do we have to?' he asked, concentrating hard on breathing deeply and not allowing the butterflies in his stomach to get the better of him.

'They're your people. They have celebrated in your honour. The least we can do in return is to give them a good show as we leave.'

They were barely above treetop height when Ra entered the turn. Elian gasped as she dipped her wingtip and powered around in a semi-circle to head back towards the village. He was sweating profusely under the thick clothing. All he wanted was to settle into a steady rhythm that his nerve-strained stomach could anticipate, and climb into cooler air. Ra's wings were beating powerfully and at a higher frequency than the previous day, but instead of gaining height, they were gaining speed.

'Start waving, Elian. Here we go.'

Elian did as he was told, waving with his left hand whilst clamping the fingers of his right hand around the saddle grip. He had no idea what Ra intended, but he felt sure his nerves would not approve.

They approached the village at the highest speed Elian had yet experienced on Ra's back, and as they did so, the dragon extended her wings to their full span. No longer beating them, she entered a shallow dive towards the crowd of people who were waving and cheering excitedly. Lower and lower they went, and it seemed to Elian that the ground began to rush past faster and faster as they descended.

An instant later they were skimming above the heads of the crowd so close that many dived to the ground for fear of the dragon crashing into them. Then Ra gently angled her wings against the airflow and Elian gasped as, without a single beat of her wings, she soared gracefully upwards, high above the village.

'*Flying lesson number one, Elian – speed can be converted into height with minimal effort.*'

They climbed and the air-rush gradually reduced until there seemed little more than a breath of a breeze. As they ran out of momentum, Ra restarted the powerful rhythm of her wingbeat and they turned and climbed northeastwards.

'You were right, Ra,' he said, grinning back at the crowd and giving a final wave. 'That was amazing! They won't forget that in a hurry. I doubt if *I* will either.'

It was a short time later, as they were crossing the far wall of the Haleen Valley, with Elian's village lost in the distance behind them, that the enormity of what he was doing began to sink in.

'Where are we going now?' he asked.

'*I told you – to Orupee to see the Oracle.*'

Orupee was hundreds, if not thousands of leagues away. To travel that far, even on a dragon, would take a considerable time: days, if not weeks. Yet they had only been flying a matter of minutes and he was already further from home than he had ever been before.

'That doesn't really mean much to me. For a start, Orupee is a huge continent – I looked on a map before we left. Whereabouts in Orupee does the Oracle live? Also, I've no idea who, or what,

63

this Oracle is. I'd like to have some idea of what we're trying to do.'

'*The Oracle is an entity that dwells in a cave hidden deep in the great mountain range of central Orupee,*' Aurora explained. '*Legend has it that the Oracle is a dragon spirit, though I would not like to vouch for the validity of that claim until I have encountered it for myself. It is said to have great powers of prophecy and knowledge, and all dragons are drawn to it at the appropriate time – normally once they have met with their dragonrider. I can feel the pull now. The sensation is strange and irresistible, but not frightening, or unpleasant.*'

'So you've never actually met this Oracle. How do you know it exists if you've never seen it?'

'*There are dragons within my enclave who have encountered the Oracle. Each described a similar encounter, though each perceived the Oracle slightly differently. Dragons do not tell lies. It is a matter of honour.*'

Elian thought for a moment, searching for a frame of reference.

'Is the Oracle a god, then? A dragon god?' he asked.

'*No, Elian, dragons do not worship the Oracle, but we do accord it our respect. It is not a creator, but for millennia the Oracle has given dragons a special sense*

64

of purpose. Many humans spend their entire lives wondering why they exist. Dragons are fortunate. We have no such unanswered questions. We spend our lives accumulating knowledge and skills against the day that the Oracle calls. When the time comes, the Oracle reveals the prophetic purpose for our lives and tells us what we must do to complete our life's mission. On completion of our task, we are left fulfilled. My elders told me of their encounters and the tasks they were given. Their accounts were fascinating. I look forward eagerly to our encounter.'

'Our encounter?' Elian asked. 'So I'm going to meet this Oracle as well?'

'Of course. We are as one now, Elian. Our bond joins us, and nothing but death can separate us. Such is the joy of the union between dragon and rider.'

Elian had doubts that he knew Aurora could feel through the bond. Although he was delighted to be Ra's rider, he was apprehensive about the prospect of searching for a dragon spirit in a distant mountain range. What would she do if they did not find this Oracle? Or worse, if she discovered the Oracle was a fake – what then?

'Do not fear, Elian. The Oracle is real. You will see.'

They continued northeast for several hours, climbing so high that Elian felt as if he should be able to see the whole world. He watched in wonder as the wide grasslands of the open savannah slipped steadily by beneath them. His gratitude for the fur-lined clothing increased quickly as they climbed. After his initial period of overheating, it did not take long for the air at the higher altitudes to send its cold fingers creeping through the layers to his body. His sweat cooled, leaving him feeling damp and uncomfortable.

By the time Ra began to descend in the late hours of the afternoon, his teeth were chattering and his flesh felt chilled through to the bone. He could no longer feel the saddle-grips through his gloves, though his fingers remained locked around them. If he had not been wearing all the heavy clothing, he would have been forced to ask Ra to take him back down into warmer air.

They landed near a large water hole. A small herd of deer scattered, nimbly bounding away at high speed as they recognised the approach of a top predator. Some headed out into the open grass-lands, whilst others raced for a nearby stand of trees, only to veer and scatter in other directions before reaching cover.

Elian did not realise how cold-soaked he was until he tried to get down from Ra's back.

'*Are you all right?*' Ra asked when he did not

move. Elian could hear the worried tones in her 'voice' as she sensed his rising panic.

'I d-d-don't know. I've never b-been this c-c-cold before.'

'Don't panic, Elian. You'll warm up quickly enough now that we're down. I'm sorry. I should have realised that you would be susceptible to the cold at the heights we were flying. Please forgive me. It will take me a while to learn my new limits now I have a rider. Can you get down? You might feel better for a drink. The water here is pure enough for you to drink if you cannot manage the stopper on your water-skin. I stopped here during my journey to find you. It is a good place to rest.'

Moving was painful, but over the following few minutes Elian slowly disentangled his feet from the stirrups. Easing his right leg over Ra's back he slid down the dragon's side to the ground. His descent was not exactly dignified, and his collapse into a heap for a second time would have been embarrassing if there had been anyone to see it.

Her head twisted around on her long neck to nuzzle him.

'I'm all right, Ra. I just need to get my blood moving again, that's all. It feels as if all my strength and co-ordination has been sucked out by the cold.'

It took two tries, but on the second attempt Elian managed to get to his feet and stagger a few steps away from the dragon. As he did so, he spotted something approaching at speed. It took a moment to register what he was looking at, and a moment more to process the information and formulate a warning. Aurora, however, was a split heartbeat ahead of him and issued a mighty roar of rage that caused all but one of the approaching men to falter for an instant.

'DRAGONHUNTERS!' she exclaimed. 'Quick! Climb up on my back, Elian. We have to get away from here as fast as we can.'

'I can't! My legs will barely move and my arms are no better. Go without me. Save yourself, Ra! It's you they're after – not me!'

'Leave you? I've only just found you. I'm not going to leave you.'

'But they'll hurt you, Ra. Maybe even kill you. Go! You must. We don't have time to argue. Go!'

The dragonhunters had cleverly approached in a semi-circle to trap Ra against the water hole, allowing her no avenue of escape unless she tried to breach the line. But Ra was not about to chance a dragonhunter's spear.

'I'll be back for you, Elian. Try to get away from them if you can. It's not their place to deny our future.'

With that she unfurled her wings, turned and hurled herself at the water hole. Elian and the dragonhunters watched in amazement as the first down-stroke of her mighty wings generated enough lift for her to skip across the surface of the water like a swan. Somehow, she managed a quick second stroke without sinking into the water, and then a third and she was clear of the water and powering up into the air.

Elian's heart pounded with relief and wonder as he watched her escape. But any thoughts he might have had of getting away himself were shattered moments later when he found himself surrounded by a large group of men armed with fearsome-looking weapons.

One man stepped forwards from the line and regarded Elian intently. He made a gesture and two other men advanced and grabbed Elian, restraining him by the upper arms.

'The dragon will return,' Kasau said quietly, but with conviction. His mismatched eyes were calm as he alternated his gaze between Elian and the distant, retreating dragon. 'We have her rider. She won't go far.'

Chapter Six

Don't Run!

'Don't run!'

For the briefest moment, Nolita hesitated in her flight towards the trees. Her stride broke into a skipping stumble as she scanned around her for the owner of the voice. There was nobody nearby. Had someone shouted? No. The voice had sounded gentle, yet strange and near, almost as if it had whispered in her ear.

It must have been my imagination, she concluded as her legs rediscovered their rhythm. She had always had vivid dreams. Some looked on such things as a blessing, but to Nolita dreaming was a curse, as her dreams usually degenerated to nightmares.

She heard the whooshing of the beast's wings as it landed behind her, but did not look round. The stream was between her and the trees. With an enormous bound, she leaped it. The pause as she hung in the air above the water seemed to last an age. When she landed her legs kicked her forwards like a startled deer, and she sped between the trees, ducking under branches and weaving between the trunks.

'*Please come back. I don't want to hurt you.*'

What was this? The voice was clearer this time. It was inside her head. She was sure of it. Was she losing her mind? Unless she thought. No! Don't be a fool, Nolita! It can't be the beast. It can't be!

'*I've waited so long to meet you, Nolita,*' the voice said softly. '*Please don't run.*'

Nolita's fear had been absolute during her first encounter with the beast, but the voice in her head added an entire new dimension to it. This was dread unlike any she had ever known before. Earlier, there had been a focus – something she could run from. But how could she run from a voice inside her head? White terror enveloped her.

Branches lashed at her arms, body and face. Bushes and undergrowth clawed at her legs. Nolita felt none of it. Uncaring of direction, she ran.

It was an unseen root that brought her flight to a sudden and undignified end. One moment she was running, the next she was flying head first through the air. Her arms waved frantically in a vain effort to control her flight, but she hit the ground hard, the wind whooshing from her lungs as her body skidded and rolled to a halt in the underbrush.

She lay there for some time, heaving and gasping in desperate shuddering breaths. The voice in her head was gone. That was one good thing. The sense of a presence she had felt when it had spoken was no longer there. However, she could still feel something – an awareness, or a link. Something. *It* had done this to her. She was sure of it. But *what* had it done?

As she slowly regained some control over her breathing, Nolita checked her body for injuries. There were a few scratches, but nothing to worry about. She was remarkably unscathed. What would have happened if she had listened to the beast, though? She shuddered at the thought.

Would it leave now that it knew she would not fall for its soft voice and its hypnotic eyes? Should she creep back and see? The villagers revered its kind. Even her mother was under the spell. She would have forbidden Nolita from running away. But if Nolita continued to run now she would not be disobeying. For some reason that felt important.

She needed provisions to survive in the wild. Maybe she could sneak back to the village in the night? No! It was too dangerous. She would keep going and do her best to live off the land. Luckily, her small water-skin was still tied to her belt. She also had her belt knife with her – something she did not always carry.

What did she need? Oiled skins to protect against the rain? More clothing? Food and more water? Maybe a bow and some arrows? All of these things could be made, caught, collected or stolen as she journeyed.

'This way is best,' she told herself. 'I'll survive, or I won't, but I'm not going back. The adults wouldn't understand. They'd lecture me on honour and my duty to the creatures and those who ride them. I'll not risk being handed over to it like a sacrificial goat.'

The great woodlands of northern Cemaria were so huge that she could walk for hundreds of leagues without ever having to leave the safety they offered. The beast was too large to follow her between the trees. If she kept her cool and stayed on the move she could hide from it for ever.

The thing that worried her most was that it had got inside her head. Her scalp itched as she thought about the beast's invasion of her thoughts. She wanted to scrub her scalp, but couldn't. Not here. The nearest water was behind her and she was not about to go back. It would have to wait a while. Besides, she knew instinctively that scrubbing her scalp and face would not remove the sensation. It was on the inside. How could she hope to clean away something that was beyond the reach of soap and water?

Brushing down her clothes with her hands, Nolita staggered to her feet. The scratches stung, and her chest and right upper arm felt bruised from her fall. Rather than ignore the pain or seek to lessen it, however, Nolita harnessed it as a focus. It helped her block out the fear. Without a backward glance, she set off at a more sensible pace between the trees. Away from home. Away from family. Away from *it*.

Chapter Seven
Kira

'Disarm the boy and bring him,' Kasau ordered.

'Yes, Kasau.'

The order was given in soft tones, but the way the hunters manhandled Elian towards the stand of trees was anything but gentle. His sword was taken from its scabbard before he even remembered it was at his side and his backpack was pulled from his shoulders. The men then alternately shoved and dragged him, as he struggled to force his limbs into action. There was no question of attempting to escape. He could no more run than he could follow Aurora by skipping across the surface of the water.

By the time they reached the edge of the small wooded area, Elian's circulation had returned and he could walk unaided. Feeling had returned to his hands and feet, and his skin in both areas felt as though it was burning; a delicious agony of pain and pleasure, as blood flooded through the outer layers of his flesh. He was led into the very centre of the stand of trees where the men had set up camp. The guards threw him to the ground next to the fire pit. Winded by the impact, it took a moment before he could roll over and push himself up into a sitting position.

Kasau wasted no time in organising his men. Elian's two guards did not leave his side, but the rest of the party gathered around at their leader's signal.

'We don't have long until nightfall,' he observed. 'We need traps set before dark sets in. My guess is that she'll approach from the east at dawn, when her powers are at their peak. We will therefore concentrate our efforts on the eastern edge.'

'What powers does she have, Kasau?'

'Do you want an honest answer?'

The man nodded. 'I've never come this close to a dawn dragon before.'

'The truth is I don't know anything for certain,' Kasau admitted. 'And what little I've heard was rumour and speculation. Does anyone here know about dawn dragons?' His question met with silence. 'You, boy – do you know what powers your dragon possesses?'

Elian met Kasau's gaze with a sullen, defiant stare. No more than a few heartbeats passed before the hunter shook his head.

'I thought not. You only met her for the first time yesterday. Why should you know? I doubt she'll use fire, even if she can project it. She'll not risk hurting her rider. Aside from that I can think of little she could do against a standard set of dragon traps. We'll prepare as best we can. Husam – you and Tembo take three men and set traps on the western edge in case she's a wily one. If we have time later, we'll set more to the north and south.'

He turned to Elian's guards. 'You two remain with the boy. Don't let him out of your sight. If he escapes, I'll personally gut you where you stand.'

There was a moment of tense silence. Kasau stared at the two guards almost as if trying to hypnotise them. Suddenly he broke eye contact and turned away. In silence he led the majority of the men off to the eastern quarter of the wood. Elian shuddered. The leader of the dragonhunters was the creepiest man he had ever seen. His mismatched eyes were strange, but it was more than that. There was an aura of coldness about him that made him almost inhuman.

It was a while before Elian dared to move. After Kasau's warning the guards looked poised to stamp on him, or worse, if he so much as twitched. With his fur-lined garments over his normal clothing, it was not long before he began to overheat in the warmth of the late afternoon. Initially he was determined not to ask for anything. However, as he began to sweat, so his headache returned. His skull throbbed and pounded until he was forced to ask for water and to take off his outer layer of clothing.

After careful consideration and a quiet, whispered conference, the guards decided to allow his requests. The water tasted brackish and stale. It quenched his immediate thirst, but he was too dehydrated for the drink to grant a quick fix to his headache. It would take time for his body to absorb the water. The best cure was sleep, but it was hard to contemplate sleep when these men were preparing to kill his dragon.

'*Don't come back for me, Ra. They're setting traps for you. Don't come back. You must stay away . . .*'

It was not much, but it was the best he could do. He repeated the warnings over and over again in his mind, concentrating through the thumping pain of his headache with dogged determination. It was hard to say exactly how long he kept it up, but the light under the trees was fading fast when Kasau appeared, as if from nowhere.

'Give it up, boy. She'll not hear you,' he said, his calm, soft voice making Elian jump guiltily.

'How did you know what I was doing?'

'It was written all over your face,' the dragon-hunter said with a shrug. 'Your mind speaking won't work over long distances. You might as well shout out loud for all the good it will do.'

'How do you know?' Elian asked.

'I've been doing this a long time. I know dragons. The mind link appears common to all types of dragon, but it normally only works over a relatively short range – a few hundred paces at most. Under exceptional circumstances I've seen it work over longer distances, but that was unusual.'

'But you told the others that you've never seen a dawn dragon before.'

Kasau's eyes went distant. 'That's true, boy. I haven't. Dawn dragons are rare – extremely rare. I wasn't even sure any existed until yesterday. To take such a beast will mark the pinnacle of my career.'

'Why are you doing this?' Elian asked. 'If you know dragons, then you know they're friendly and intelligent. Aurora is good and noble. She hasn't hurt anyone. And you know the Overlords don't allow the hunting of dragons, except for rogues. Even night dragons are protected. I don't know what the punishment is for killing a dragon, but I expect it's unpleasant.'

'Death, boy. The penalty is death. As for why we're doing it – the answer should be obvious. Gold. What else?'

'You'd risk your life to kill an intelligent creature for a few gold pieces? That's sick!' Elian exclaimed, unable to contain his horror.

'No, I wouldn't do it for a few gold pieces, boy. But that golden dragon of yours is worth more than a few gold pieces. Magicians will pay more gold than you could possibly imagine for a single piece of horn from a dawn dragon. Every part of her is saleable: the scales, the bones, the eyes, the talons, the teeth – everything. The beast is worth a fortune greater than any of the Overlords will ever possess. Tell me that's not worth the risk.'

Elian didn't answer. He could believe what Kasau said about Aurora's worth, but there was an edge in the man's voice. The dragonhunter was hiding something. He talked of the gold, but there was no passion in his voice as he did so. Whatever his motive for wanting to kill Aurora, it was not the money. Elian was sure of it.

Was he a man who killed for the sake of killing? Did he get some perverse pleasure from killing a creature that nature had made larger, stronger and faster than himself? Or was it something else? Whatever his motive, Elian could see that Kasau would not be turned by anything a young dragon-rider said.

The dragonhunter did not seem concerned by Elian's silence.

'I'm going to tie you up now, boy,' he said. 'I'll not risk my men making a foolish error that might allow you to slip away. We'll be lighting the fire shortly, so you won't freeze. Now put your hands behind your back.'

Elian stared defiantly into the man's strange eyes and did not move.

'We can do this the easy way, or the hard way,' Kasau said, his soft voice impassive as he met Elian's stare with a cold, heartless expression. 'It's your choice. I care not.'

The dragonhunter pulled a length of cord from a pocket and wound one end around each hand to form a garrotte. Elian maintained his stare for another few heartbeats before relenting with a sigh. He placed his hands meekly behind his back.

'Ah, you do have some intelligence then. That's good. I like to see that in a boy.'

With swift efficiency, Kasau tied Elian's hands together. Despite Elian's best efforts to work some slack into the cord as the dragonhunter bound him, subsequent testing proved the knots to be well tied. Kasau then bound Elian's ankles together, and pushed him to the ground. A third piece of cord was used to join the two sets of knots together. He left about a handspan of cord running between the wrist and ankle knots, allowing Elian some flexibility to alter his position, but not much.

By the time Kasau had finished, Elian realised that although he could manoeuvre his body to lie on one side or the other, he could not roll through a full three hundred and sixty degrees. He was helpless. Within moments the shame and frustration of his situation built within him until tears began to well. He had been a dragonrider for a day and already he had failed Aurora so badly that she might die.

'Give it up, boy,' Kasau ordered. 'There's nothing you can do. Get some rest. It'll be over soon enough. When we have your dragon, you'll be released.'

Elian did not believe Kasau for a heartbeat. The dragonhunters could not let him go. Once they had killed Ra, they would have no choice but to kill him as well. He had to escape. It was easy enough said, but how?

Darkness fell swiftly under the leafy canopy. Dusk had barely settled before the blanket of night smothered the campsite. The guards lit the fire and sat idly chatting about how they would spend their fortunes, whilst Elian secretly worked to free his hands and feet.

Throughout the evening he felt the ground around him for a stone with a sharp edge, or anything that he might use to cut through the cord. Pretending to seek a more comfortable position was not difficult, for in reality he never achieved one. He moved frequently, shuffling his body a little at a time to extend his search, but he found nothing. Hiding his straining muscles from the guards with careful body positioning, he flexed against the cord until the pain became unbearable. He tried so hard he felt sure he was in danger of breaking his wrists, but the cords remained as tight as ever.

Eventually, late into the night, exhaustion caught up with him and he slipped into a troubled sleep. Waking with a start, the first thing Elian noticed was that his hands and feet were totally numb, as was the whole of his right arm from having slept on it for some hours.

'*Be strong, Elian. We'll be together soon.*'

It was Ra! She was nearby.

'*No, Ra! You mustn't! They've set traps for you. They'll kill you. Please stay away,*' he thought, focusing hard to project his words loud and clear.

Even as he completed the thought, he noticed Kasau silently waking those men still under blankets.

'She's back,' he whispered as he shook them. 'Get to your positions.'

If he had not been so frantic with worry, Elian would probably have admired the men for their response. They melted into the trees in the pre-dawn half-light without a sound. Having roused his men, Kasau made a final check on Elian's bonds.

'It won't be long now,' he said, his soft voice tight with suppressed excitement.

'I hope you rot in hell!' Elian responded, spitting at the man's back as he turned to follow his men towards the eastern edge of the woods.

Kasau did not look back. Within a few heartbeats he was gone, leaving Elian all alone next to the smouldering fire pit. 'Why haven't the dragon-hunters left a guard?' he wondered aloud. 'Because I've already served my purpose,' he breathed. 'Ra's back and I haven't managed to get loose. They're right. Why should I suddenly be able to get away now?'

'Because you have help,' whispered a voice right next to his ear.

Elian nearly jumped out of his skin. 'Who—?'

'Shh!'

It was a girl! Who was she, and why was she

helping him? He felt the cord tying his wrists to his ankles part with a jerk and he stretched out his legs, luxuriating in the relative freedom. She cut the cords binding his wrists next, followed swiftly by those around his ankles. Within a matter of heartbeats he was free, but he could not move.

'Come on! Quickly! We've got to get out of here!' she urged.

'I can't. My feet are numb, and my legs are cramping. I don't think I can walk,' he replied, deeply shamed by his weakness.

'Here, take my arm,' she offered. 'I'll try to support you, but we have to move now. Aurora won't be able to buy us much time.'

'How do you know Aurora's name? Who are you?'

'I'm Kira; and my dragon, Longfang, told me. No more questions. There'll be time for that later. Come. We must go.'

She was a dragonrider! Elian grabbed his fur-lined gear, which was in a convenient pile within arm's reach. He shoved the hat on his head, fumbled the jacket on, stuffed the gloves clumsily into the jacket pockets, tucked the trousers under his right arm and slung his pack over his shoulder. There was no sign of his sword anywhere, but while having a weapon might have brought comfort, he knew nothing of fighting with a blade. If the hunters found him holding a sword they would be more likely to kill him. He was better off without it, he decided.

The blood was returning to his hands and feet, and the pain it brought with it was excruciating. Kira dragged him to his feet, pulling his left arm around her shoulders and tucking her right arm around his waist. Without her support he would have collapsed in an instant.

In the shadowy half-light, Elian could see she was almost as tall as he was; slim, but with surprising strength for one with such a slight build.

'Come on! Come on!' she whispered through gritted teeth, as she all but carried him off into the trees. From what he could tell they were moving just north of westwards.

Elian did his best to comply. Behind them Ra roared a challenge from some distance to the east of the woods. With the racket she was making, it would be hard for the dragonhunters to ignore her.

'Whatever you do, don't look back,' Kira warned.

'What about the traps?'

'Let me worry about those. I know where they are. Fang is waiting for us just beyond the western edge of the trees.'

With feeling returning to his extremities and the pain receding with every stride, Elian progressively leaned less on Kira. His hands and feet felt as if they were being repeatedly pricked with a million needles whilst roasting in a hot oven, but he knew the sensation would pass. By the time they reached the outer edge of the woods the worst of it was over, but to Elian's dismay Kira's dragon was nowhere to be seen.

A sudden bright flare from behind lit the countryside around them with an extraordinary golden light. Cries of wonder from the dragonhunters quickly turned to yowls of dismay and pain. Elian began to turn, but Kira stopped him.

'Don't look. If you do, you won't be able to see properly for a long time. Come on. Let's get out of here. Give me a moment and I'll give you a hand up.'

She unhooked his arm from round her neck and, to Elian's total astonishment, she seemed to climb into the air in front of him. He blinked in amazement as she twisted into a sitting position seemingly suspended in midair. She offered him her hand.

'Come on. What are you waiting for? Fang says we must go. Now! The strange one has realised you've gone. He's coming.'

Still not quite believing his eyes, Elian grabbed

her hand and tentatively raised his foot only to find what he thought to be thin air was in fact solid dragon. The camouflage was superb. He could have walked within a handspan of Longfang and never seen him. A few mind-boggling heartbeats later he was seated behind Kira. He could feel the ridge between them, but even holding it, he could not see the dragon.

'Have you ridden bareback before?' Kira whispered.

'Once.'

'Well hold tight then. A dusk dragon's best defence is its camouflage. It's effective, but flying when you can't see your ride takes a bit of getting used to.'

Elian did not doubt it. He felt himself lifted higher as Longfang stood up. Then they turned away from the line of the trees and Kira glanced back over her shoulder.

'Here we go,' she warned.

Elian's recent experience flying on Aurora proved invaluable during the next few heartbeats. The initial surge of acceleration was abrupt, but familiar. He felt the first downward sweep of the dragon's wings and a sense of exultation rushed through his stomach. They had done it. They had escaped the dragonhunters.

Chapter Eight
A Brave Flight

Husam's skin prickled as Kasau appeared next to him at the eastern edge of the woods. He had not heard the hunter approaching. How did the man move so silently? The ground was littered with twigs and leaves, but Kasau seemed able to breeze across any surface as if walking on air. It was eerie.

The golden dawn dragon paced back and forth about a hundred paces from the tree line, just out of range for a spear throw. This dragon is either very canny, or very stupid, he thought. She turned again, lashing her tail with anger and apparent frustration. It was unusual. She had drawn attention to herself, allowing them time to get into position. Most dragons would have charged into the trees by now.

'She's waiting for the sun to rise,' he heard Kasau

whisper. 'Whatever she's going to do, she'll do it as the sun breaks the horizon.'

The moment was imminent. The eastern sky was brightening by the heartbeat.

'Another dragon!'

Kasau's exclamation was little more than a whisper, but it caught Husam's attention. His head turned instantly to see where Kasau was looking. The strange hunter had stiffened, but to Husam's surprise his eyes did not appear to be focused. It was as if he were in a trance.

The hairs on the back of Husam's neck prickled again and he instinctively made a warding gesture he had been taught as a child.

'Gods, but this is a wily one!' Kasau breathed. 'She's not coming in after her rider. She's got someone else to do it for her.'

Suddenly Kasau's eyes refocused and his head whipped round. His gaze pierced Husam with a chilling intensity.

'Husam – you're with me. Bring Tembo. Quickly!'

Husam had more sense than to question the order. He scrambled through the undergrowth to where Tembo was waiting.

'She's beginning to glow!' the big man said in a hoarse whisper. 'Look, Husam. Can you see? Isn't she beautiful?'

Husam did cast a lightning glance at the dragon. Tembo was right. It was almost as if the dragon were beginning to illuminate from within, but he knew better than to get distracted.

'Tembo, we have to go. Kasau wants us. Now. Bring your weapons.'

The big man grumbled for a moment, but did as he was told. Soon the two were racing through the trees towards the campsite. When they arrived, they found Kasau examining the remains of the cords with which he had tied the young dragonrider. The cords had been cut. No dragon could do such a thing. This was the work of a human accomplice.

'This way,' Kasau said softly. 'Be ready. There's another dragon nearby.'

'How—?' Tembo began.

Husam signalled his friend to silence and they moved to follow Kasau. From behind them a sudden flare of light blazed, dividing into slices of golden fire through the trees. An instant later there followed cries of pain and dismay from their fellow hunters. Husam and Tembo instinctively turned. By chance, they were both in the shade of trees as they looked towards the light. Had the tree trunks not shielded them, they would have been temporarily blinded. When Husam checked to see if Kasau had been less fortunate, he was amazed to find that the strange man had not stopped. The quiet hunter had kept his focus ahead and was still moving forwards.

'Just inhuman!' he marvelled as he and Tembo did their best to catch up with Kasau's silent charge through the trees.

They reached the edge of the woods and for a moment Husam thought he was witnessing some sort of powerful witchcraft. The young dragonrider was floating in midair behind a girl of similar age. Beneath them the air shimmered like a heat-haze as they accelerated away from the stand of trees.

Kasau did not pause. He ran forwards and launched his spear in a mighty throw towards the escaping prisoner and his rescuer. It arced high into the air, almost seeming to hang in the sky before slowly dipping point downwards and plummeting towards its target.

The spear missed the two human figures, but struck the hazy blur beneath and behind them. A mighty roar of pain split the air and a charcoal-grey dragon materialised from the haze. The spear was stuck firmly in its flank. The two riders turned and looked down at the spear. Even at this range, Husam could see the horror on their faces. It was not a mortal wound, but the spear had penetrated deep through the dragon's scales.

They were airborne and climbing now, well

beyond spear range. Kasau turned and made eye contact first with Husam, and then with Tembo.

'Why are you still holding spears?' he asked, his soft voice dangerous and his strange eyes flashing with anger. 'We could have brought that dragon down there and then. Don't you want to be rich? The stakes just increased. Instead of one rare dragon, we're now hunting two.'

'But the dusk dragon has a rider . . .'

'As does the dawn dragon. Did that stop us? Are you blind? The dusk dragon's rider is also very young. The dusk dragon enclave is thousands of leagues away. What are the odds that she's already been there and back? Virtually nil. That means both riders are unknown to their enclaves. The risks involved in hunting two dragons are little greater than in hunting one. What were you thinking of?'

Neither Husam nor Tembo answered, but both had similar thoughts. Yes, the stakes were greater, but so was their unease with Kasau's leadership. He was hiding something. How had he known of the second dragon? Was he a shaman or a wizard? What was his secret?

Is it too late to pull out? Husam wondered to himself. But they had restrained the young dragon-rider with a view to killing his dragon. That alone was a capital offence. Now Kasau had wounded a

second dragon that had a rider. They were commit-
ted. It would be best to make the kills quickly and
move on before anyone discovered the truth.

The dusk dragon turned and flew back towards
them, meeting up with the dawn dragon overhead,
way up out of reach of any weapon.

'Go and gather the others,' Kasau ordered, his
eyes following the path of the two dragons. 'We
need to break camp quickly. They're heading
north. There's nothing in that direction but open
savannah. The dusk dragon won't fly far with that
wound. If we ride hard, we can end this tonight.'

Fang's roar of pain and his loss of camouflage sent
fear deep into Elian's heart. When he looked back
and saw the weapon sticking out of the dragon's
thigh, his heart sank. Would Fang be able to fly?

Then they were airborne and climbing, and
Elian saw Kasau with two other hunters, watching
them. Even though they were a good distance away,
Elian fancied he could see Kasau's expression of
frustration. As they gained height, they circled back
towards the woods. They passed over the treetops
safely above the reach of the most powerful of
bows. As they did so, Aurora drew in alongside
them and the two dragons turned north.

'Are you all right, Elian?'

'I'm fine, thanks, Ra,' he thought back. 'But Fang's hurt. Can you tell how bad it is?'

'It's not good. The weapon moves in the wound with every wingbeat. He's in a lot of pain.'

'Is there anything we can do?' Elian asked anxiously.

'We? No, but there are those who can,' Ra answered. 'For now Fang will concentrate on getting as far from the hunters as he can. There will be time to arrange healing later.'

'While I was escaping with Kira there was a flood of light. What did you do?' he asked.

'Let's just say that I gave the hunters a glimpse of my full glory,' Ra replied cryptically.

Hearing Ra's thoughts was reassuring. Despite her obvious concern for Fang's wound, she sounded unflustered. Her calm, matter-of-fact voice in his head gave Elian a warm feeling of safety, though he knew they were not out of danger yet.

The dragons beat a measured time with their wings, and the further they flew, the more Elian's heart soared. The wind-rush in his ears and the feel of it combing his hair felt even more special today than it had on his first flight. They did not climb very high, as neither Kira nor Elian were dressed to survive the cold. It seemed to Elian that they were flying faster than they had yesterday. At their

95

current speed he felt they should be safe from the hunters in quick time.

'It's a visual illusion, Elian,' Ra explained. 'When we were up high your field of view was far greater. Down here we cannot see as far, so the ground appears to rush past faster. We're actually flying far slower than we did the other day.'

'Oh, right. I see,' Elian replied, feeling rather foolish.

After a short while he tapped Kira on the shoulder, thinking to thank her properly. She twisted to see what he wanted.

It was the first time Elian had seen Kira's face clearly. Instantly, he realised she was a tribeswoman. Four circular white paint dots described a shallow concave arc under each of her eyes. Below the dots a diagonal slash of bright red paint ran downwards and outwards across her cheeks. Elian did not know enough about the southern tribes to identify the markings. Her thick black hair was drawn back and plaited. Deep brown eyes framed by long dark lashes regarded him with an expectant gaze.

'Kira, I just wanted to say thank you,' he began. 'I'm sorry I wasn't more help. I owe you.'

'Don't thank me,' she replied. 'I didn't want to get involved. Fang insisted. Now he's hurt. Do you know that when your dragon is hurt, you feel his pain? I'm beginning to understand exactly what being a dragonrider means.' Her voice held no warmth.

'No, I didn't know the bond worked that way. I'm sorry. Have you been with Fang long?' Elian realised as soon the question left his lips that he was asking the obvious, and he mentally kicked himself. In her current mood, Kira's reaction was predictable and instant.

'What do you think?' she snapped. 'Do I look like I'm an old hand? If you must know, I first met with him about ten days ago.'

'Then you *are* an old hand,' Elian said, with a grin meant to disarm. 'I only met Ra two days ago.'

Kira ignored his peace effort, her eyes going distant. Her voice was cold with bitterness as she continued. 'I kept our bonding a secret for two days, but it couldn't last. Eventually Fang insisted I leave to find something called the Oracle. I was three days from home when Aurora called for help. I was surprised when Fang agreed. All he'd talked about was getting to the Oracle quickly, yet as soon as Aurora called he insisted we come.'

Elian felt her accusatory gaze burning into him, but he did not want to show further weakness by looking away. Chance had brought them together. They were both facing similar challenges. A *difficulty shared is more easily overcome*, his mother had always said. But above all, he needed a friend now he was a long way from home.

Kira seemed full of fearless bravery and fiery, passionate emotion. Her feistiness and strength of character made the girls from his village seem meek by comparison. If he could win her friendship, she would prove a useful ally.

'We could travel together for a while, if you like,' he offered, working hard to keep his voice mellow and determinedly ignoring her hostility. 'Ra and I were also on our way to see the Oracle when the hunters trapped me. Maybe we should share what we know.'

'Really? Has Ra told you anything about the Oracle?' she asked, her curiosity tweaked. 'Do you know what it is?'

'Ra did tell me a little. From what I understand, the Oracle is some sort of dragon spirit. When we meet it, the Oracle will give her – us – a mission. Apparently Ra has been preparing for this mission all her life. Once we complete it, Ra can live out the rest of her life feeling fulfilled. I imagine it'll be the same for Fang. Does that make any sense?'

His explanation took some of the anger from Kira's eyes. He could almost see the thought processes whirling through her mind.

'Yes, I think it does. But what will we do then? What are we supposed to do when this life mission is complete?' she asked, her tone still sour.

'I don't know,' Elian admitted. 'I hadn't thought that far ahead. I intend to concentrate on one thing at a time. Get the mission out of the way, then—'

'Of course, we have to *reach* the Oracle first,' Kira snapped. She looked down meaningfully and Elian automatically followed her gaze to the spear. 'He's bleeding badly and the effort of carrying two is tiring him fast. We'll have to land soon.'

'If we could just find some broadleaf rockcrop,' Elian said thoughtfully. 'The juice of the leaves helps stop bleeding. It works with people, so I assume it'll work with dragons. If we can find something to numb the pain as well . . .'

'Broadleaf rockcrop?' she asked. 'What does it look like?'

'At this height, we'd never spot it. When we land I'll take Ra and look for some. It's a common plant and it's a good time of year for it. We should be able to find it.

'*Ra, are you familiar with this plant?*'

Elian did his best to conjure up as vivid an image as he could in his mind.

'*Dragons have little time for plant life, Elian,*' Ra

99

replied, sounding genuinely insulted by his suggestion. '*I might take a second glance at a large bush if I thought it was concealing prey, but I generally leave the green stuff for those at the lower end of the food chain.*'

Elian smiled at her phrasing, but discarded any thoughts of sending her down to low level to search on her own. He did not want to upset her. Instead he concentrated on looking ahead at the landscape.

Ideally, he would love to have seen a natural barrier like the Haleen Rift Valley with its great escarpment to put between them and the hunters, but the land ahead was flat, open savannah. There were the purple hints of mountains in the far distance to their right, but Fang was in no fit state to fly so far.

The brave dragon flew on for over two hours before beginning his descent. Ra had spotted a water hole ahead, and told Fang to land. She judged they had travelled far enough to render another attack unlikely today.

Side by side, the dragons descended in a shallow glide and landed near the water's edge. There were a few scrubby bushes, but unlike their last stop there were no trees for enemies to hide in. The long grass of the savannah concealed many predators and game, but there were no signs of human life.

Any predators would keep their distance from the dragons. They were safe – for now.

Chapter Nine
Fish on a Hook

How many days had it been? Six? Seven? Nolita had lost count, but she knew that unless she got lucky, she would not survive much longer. Although she was reasonable at the basics of woodcraft – she could build shelters and light fires – she had never been good at hunting. Now her belly ached for food and her limbs felt weak.

Edible plantlife was not easy to find in the forest. Berries and nuts would not come into season for some time yet, and there was little else apart from fungi. But she was wary of eating any mushrooms. A boy in the village had nearly died the previous year after mistakenly eating a poisonous variety. Her best chance of finding food was to make a kill, but so far she had enjoyed no luck.

She made a portable trap that she set every night,

but no animal had been foolish enough to step into it. Her brother was an expert at setting traps and snares, but Nolita had never worked out what he did to gain such consistent success. If she were to stay in one place for more than a night, then she could set more snares and build more traps, but she had been forced to keep on the move. IT had been following her.

At first she had thought it was her overactive imagination at work, but then the beast had spoken in her mind again and she knew for certain that it had not given up. How it was following her was not clear. Surely it was impossible for it to see her through the thick tree canopy, yet somehow it had found her every day and plagued her mind with its soft voice and its cajoling words.

Nolita was descending a steep slope, pondering different ways she might shake the beast from her trail. The footing was slippery and dangerous. Her head and eyes were fixed downwards on the ground immediately ahead when a snarling noise stopped her in her tracks. There was no mistaking the sound. Legs frozen in place, she raised her head slowly and met the eyes of the wolf. It was no more than a dozen paces away. Its body was dipped forwards on its extended front legs, and its hackles were up as it deepened its snarl into a rich, throaty growl.

With a great effort of will, Nolita broke eye contact with it and flicked her gaze around to see if any more were lurking nearby. It appeared to be alone. Relief warmed her as she met its intent stare again. A lone wolf was dangerous, but not as dangerous as a hunting pack. Her stomach fluttered with fear, but it was nothing compared to the terror that had consistently haunted her for the last few days.

Under different circumstances Nolita might have tried to run, but she knew that to do so would likely provoke an attack. A wolf's killing tactic was normally to hamstring its victim as it ran. Having immobilised its prey it would then go for the throat. By standing her ground, the wolf would be forced to think twice about attacking.

Nolita slowly moved her right hand until it rested on the handle of her belt knife. The wolf's growl deepened still further and its body weaved on the spot as it threatened to leap forwards. She drew her blade, the bright flash of steel strengthening her feeling of control over the situation.

'Leave me alone,' she said aloud. The words had no confidence in them, but to her surprise they had the desired effect. The wolf gave one final snarl, then turned and trotted away across the slope. 'I suppose there must be plenty of easier game out here,' Nolita muttered. 'I just wish I could hunt well enough to be so choosy.'

'That was bravely done, Nolita. Come to me and you'll not have to worry about wolves or hunting. No predator will dare threaten you with me around and I'll bring you meat to eat whenever you want it. I'm a very accomplished hunter.'

'Gods, no!' she exclaimed, instantly beginning to skip down the steep hillside at a speed that she would never normally attempt. 'Not again!' she muttered in terror. 'How do you keep finding me?'

'We are bonded. I'm drawn to you. It is our destiny to be together.'

For a moment Nolita was speechless. The last thing she had expected was an answer. How had it heard what she had said? She had barely breathed the question. It was impossible. She skidded to a stop against a thick tree trunk.

'What if I don't want to be bonded?' she asked more loudly, forcing herself to look up at the tree-tops to see if she could see any sign of the beast overhead.

'You have no choice. I have no choice. It is our destiny. I don't know why. It just is. Please don't be afraid. I intend you no harm. I am Firestorm, your dragon.'

A towering wall of fear was forming again. Was there no escape? 'There are always choices,' she

105

shouted, trying to use her anger and feelings of violation as a focus to overcome the terror that threatened to crush her chest. 'I don't want any part of your destiny! *I* control my life. Me! Not you. Not my mother. Not destiny. Me. I don't want any part of you, beast. Go! Leave me alone.'

'*You cannot turn me aside like you did the wolf, Nolita. We must go together. The Oracle is calling. It is our time.*'

'There is no "we", do you hear? I'll never go anywhere with you.'

Sobs of fear and anger ripped through Nolita. She pushed away from the tree to begin skipping and galloping downwards, using gravity to lend her energy. Teetering on the edge of control she fended off saplings and swung under low branches. Her legs felt heavy and wooden as she reached the bottom of the wooded valley. Running here was impossible. Nolita did not have the strength left, but she gritted her teeth and staggered onwards as fast as she could.

With tears streaking her cheeks, Nolita managed no more than a hundred paces before she was forced to slow. Time blurred the following hour into a seemingly endless alternation between walking and a stumbling jog. For all she could remember, Nolita could have been running minutes, hours, or days.

It was the sound of running water that brought her back to her senses. The instant she heard the bubbling song of the stream, Nolita was gripped by an overwhelming urge to wash. She had no soap, but that was not important. It was the process: the feel of water, the rubbing, the motion and the sensation of cleanliness. The ritual would help bring her out of the darkness.

The sound was not difficult to trace, for it was a large stream. With grateful sobs of relief, Nolita staggered to the mossy bank and fell to her knees. She drove her hands into the water and began to scrub frantically at her palms and fingers. With methodical diligence and broken fingernails she rubbed and scratched at the ingrained dirt. She washed and washed until her hands were frozen and shrivelled. Then she leaned over the edge of the stream and dipped her head into the chill water. The cold took her breath away, but she did not flinch. With vigorous thoroughness she washed her scalp, hair and face.

The cold water and the familiar ritual calmed her. As she leaned back to squeeze the water from her hair, her eyes automatically followed a fish darting through the pool and across to hide under the far bank. A horrible thought struck her. She was like a fish on a hook. She could run until she was unable to run any more, but the invisible line tying her to the beast would still be there. Unless she could break the link somehow, the beast would eventually drag her in. The calm that had settled over her shattered like smashed ice.

'There's got to be a way out. There's just got to be,' she whispered.

Chapter Ten
Through the Gateway

Elian dismounted, removed his heavy jacket and hat, and went off to search out the broadleaf rock-crop. It did not take him long to find an armload of the fleshy leaves. When he returned, Kira was staring at Fang's wound, furious.

'Look at this! Look what those barbarians are using to hunt with,' she stormed, beckoning.

At close range it was easy to see why the weapon jutting from the dragon's flank had not worked loose during the flight. It had wicked barbs carved into the point to ensure that it snagged in the victim's flesh. To pull it free would cause more damage. He was appalled.

'The women of our village use this to treat bad wounds,' he said. 'The juice slows bleeding. Let's hope it works on dragons.'

Elian folded the leaves into a tight bundle and then twisted until milky-white sap began to seep from the wad of green. He dribbled the fluid into the top of the wound, working hard to extract every last drop by twisting and retwisting the leaves.

Gently, he changed the angle of the spear in the wound to allow the juice of the leaves to penetrate as deeply as possible. Fang let out a long sigh of pain. But Elian's joy, the sap acted quickly and the blood flow slowed to a trickle.

'I don't think we should take out the spear until we have something to help block Fang's pain,' he suggested. '*And his rider's,*' he added silently.

Kira's eyes went distant for a moment and Elian realised she was relaying this information to her dragon.

'Fang says to go ahead and remove it. He promises not to flinch.'

'You want *me* to do it?' he asked, surprised.

'You seem to know what you're doing,' she replied defensively. 'I'm not good with this sort of thing.'

Elian held her gaze for a moment. The barriers were still up behind her eyes, but he was not blind to the opportunity she was offering. This was a chance to impress – a chance to show his worth. But when he pulled the spear free, she would feel Fang's pain. He was not sure he wanted to cause her any more hurt.

'*You will do fine, Elian. Remove the weapon. It is giving Fang a lot of discomfort. Kira is strong. They will both recover quickly once it's out. Tomorrow we will seek a day dragon and arrange for the wound to be fully healed,*' Ra interjected.

'So it's true then?' he asked aloud. 'Day dragons have healing powers? Brilliant!'

Kira, who was still staring at him, raised her eyebrows in surprise. 'What's that?'

'*I'm surprised at you, Elian. I thought you knew this, at least, of dragonlore. Day dragons are fire breathers, but dragonfire does not always burn. They can use their fire for healing if so moved. Tomorrow we shall seek a day dragon who is willing to breathe a healing flame over Longfang's wound.*'

'I can see three-way conversations are going to get a bit annoying!' Elian said, looking up at the sky in frustration. 'Kira, Aurora says that we're going to look for a day dragon tomorrow. Apparently day dragons can breathe healing fire.'

He turned to his dragon and spoke aloud for Kira's benefit. 'Ra, I told you I don't know much about dragons ... but I do know something about herb lore. Dragons aren't the only ones with useful skills. Watch.' He turned and looked Longfang in

111

the eye. 'I appreciate your bravery, Fang, but it's unnecessary. I noticed some ripe peppers growing not far away. As the broadleaf worked on you, I think that rubbing cut pepper into your wound will work to numb the pain as well. Give me a minute.'

Kira's eyes had gone wide with stunned shock when Elian had addressed Ra with a tone other than worshipful respect. That he went on to address her dragon in the same manner left her speechless. Silently she relayed his words to Fang as Elian marched off and recovered several peppers. When he returned, he used Kira's belt knife to split them lengthways into quarters. He scraped out the pips, then rubbed the moist interior of the pepper around and into the wound as best he could. Longfang's leg twitched several times, but considering how painful it must have been, Elian marvelled at the dragon's self-control.

After allowing some time for the numbing effect of the pepper sap to take hold, he took hold of the spear and braced himself against the dragon's haunch. If he had been able, he would have tried to cut or break off the barbs before removing the spear. But Ra said this was impossible, as the spear's tip was made of dragon horn, a substance far harder than any metal. Instead, Elian was forced to use Kira's belt knife again – this time to slice a clean path through the dragon's flesh for the barbs to pass. Even so, withdrawing the spear was not easy and the sucking, tearing noise it made as he pulled it free was horrible.

Kira stood by the entire time, anxiously watching as Elian worked. When he finally managed to remove the spear there were tears in her eyes.

'Fang says to thank you for your gentle touch. He felt very little pain,' she said.

'*That was well done, Elian.*' There was pride in Ra's tone.

Elian nodded. He felt sick. From his perspective there had been nothing gentle in what he had done. He had never had to deal with such a nasty wound before. It had felt more like butchering raw meat than anything connected with healing. He squeezed more of the milky broadleaf sap into the now gaping wound and the fresh flood of blood gradually slowed to a trickle. It looked a mess, but it was the best he could do. They could not bandage the dragon's thigh – it was so big that any material they could cobble together from the clothes they were wearing would not be sufficient.

'*Do dragons ever lie on their backs, or their sides?*' Elian asked Ra silently.

'*Not very often – it's most uncomfortable,*' she replied.

'Can you ask Fang to roll over onto his left side, please? He'll need to stay that way as long as he can stand it.'

'Might I ask why?' Ra inquired loftily.

'The bleeding will slow if his heart is lower than the wound. It'll allow a scab to form more easily.'

'Oh! Very well then.'

Kira looked momentarily surprised and worried to see Fang rolling over, but a quick mental exchange with him put her at ease again. After giving him an affectionate pat on the neck, she turned to Elian, and he could see the cold barrier settle back into her eyes.

'Come,' she ordered. 'Let's find something to eat.'

Elian nodded. He was a bit peeved that she had not offered a word of thanks on her own behalf, but he buried his disappointment deep inside. It was a long way to central Orupee. There would be plenty of time for her to get to know and like him.

They moved a short distance from Fang and cleared a space on the ground to make a fire not far from the water's edge. Elian gathered some rocks and placed them in a small circle, leaving a gap on the windward side for air to feed the fire.

Kira scavenged for material to burn. There was not much around. A dead bush offered enough kindling and wood to build a short-lived fire. They set to work breaking and sorting the wood from the bush into piles of thin twigs for kindling, small sticks to build a base, and larger sticks. The small stuff would be great for lighting and establishing a flame, whilst the thicker bits would fuel it for a while. When he saw how little they had, Elian offered to take Ra on a quick trip to the nearest trees to get some proper logs.

'Do it after we've eaten,' Kira replied. 'We won't be able to move again today. Fang needs to recover. We've got plenty of time before dark.'

She was right. A short while later, they had water boiling in a small copper pan from Elian's backpack over a crackling flame that danced and popped as it hungrily consumed their stockpile of sticks. The dry wood gave off little smoke, but the smell of it was heavenly.

Elian cut a potato into small pieces and added it to the water with a few pinches of dried herbs. Kira took an apple from her pack and diced it in similar fashion, adding it to the broth with some ground sweetroot. Each let out sighs of contentment as they took their first taste.

In the afternoon he rode off on Ra to collect wood for a more substantial fire to keep them warm through the night. In the meantime, Kira roamed the immediate area in search of edible plants.

After her trip to scavenge for firewood with Elian, Ra went off hunting alone. Her trip was successful and she returned clutching a whole antelope in her talons. When she and Fang had eaten their fill, they left a succulent rear leg for the two riders. It was huge, with so much meat on the bone that the meal was like a feast. Elian and Kira roasted strips over the open flames in the early evening half-light.

Although Elian and Kira spent the evening sitting opposite one another at the fire, conversation was sparse. Elian tried a few times to spark her into talking, but she seemed to have a way of killing any topic with her first response. The spells of silence felt awkward to Elian, but not hostile. In the end he gave up and leaned back against a rock, gazing up at the millions of stars that lit up the cloudless night sky.

It was one of the clearest nights he had ever seen. The chirruping chorus of crickets blended with the nocturnal noises of amphibians, building in a slow crescendo until the occasional snap and crackle of the fire was all but lost. The air felt swollen with sound. A combination of wafting wood-smoke and the aroma of leftover roasted meat mixed with the earthy, grassy smell of the savannah. The scent filled Elian with a sense of warmth and adventure. Thoughts of danger and his trauma at the hands of the hunters faded. As his eyes relaxed their focus, the brightest stars seemed to fly down and surround him. It was a magical feeling.

Elian was not aware of drifting off to sleep, but when he woke, he did so with a start. It was before dawn and still quite dark. The fire had burned out and he felt cold, stiff and slightly damp.

'*Get up, Elian. The hunters are here. We must go.*'

'You're sure? How close are they?' he whispered. 'Will Fang be able to fly?'

'*He will have to. They're close. Gather your things. Get Kira. I will carry you both. Try not to make any noise.*'

'Where are you? I can't see you.' Elian rubbed his eyes and scanned the area around the water hole. The pre-dawn glow was just beginning to light the eastern sky.

'*I'm here.*'

A large shadowy head suddenly appeared out of what looked like thin air. Elian blinked a few times to make sure his eyes were not deceiving him, but then realised what had happened. From where he was, Ra was behind Fang, who had automatically camouflaged himself on sensing danger. The angle between Elian and Ra meant that most of the dawn dragon was shielded behind Fang's invisible body. The result looked bizarre.

'I see you,' Elian hissed.

He scrambled silently over to where Kira was sleeping and gently placed a hand on her shoulder. Her response was so fast that he did not see her move. Before Elian realised what had happened she had her knife blade pressed against his throat. For an instant he froze, frightened that any move he made might cause her to use the knife.

'Back off!' she growled, her voice soft and dangerous.

'Relax, Kira!' he whispered anxiously. 'It's me. The hunters have found us again. We need to go. Aurora will carry us both.'

Kira did not need telling twice. She was up in an instant, the knife disappearing as fast as it had appeared. Sure-footed and silent, she did not take long to gather her belongings. Elian was not so fast, but he managed to find his things without making much noise and together they moved around the invisible Longfang to where Ra was waiting.

'*Which way should we launch?*' Elian asked silently.

'*Take your pick,*' Ra offered.

'*What do you mean?*'

'*I mean it will make no difference, Elian. We're surrounded.*'

*

118

'I have you now,' Kasau breathed, pleasure coursing through his tired body. 'Your glowing hide won't save you this time.'

They had pushed the horses to the limit, riding with minimal breaks throughout the day and on through the night. Despite the bright, starlit sky, the going was slow once darkness fell. Even at a walk it took only a single unfortunate step for a horse to fall lame, or worse.

Some of the hunters had questioned the sense of taking such risks, but Kasau brushed aside their concerns and pushed them on. He knew this was likely to be their last opportunity to kill the dawn dragon before she and her rider flew beyond their ability to catch up. The hunters were all in position. The signal had been given. Each of them was armed with a weapon tipped with dragonhorn, the only substance hard enough to penetrate a dragon's scales with ease. Dragonhunters of old had hunted with swords and spears made of metal and stone. The chances of surviving an encounter with weapons of such materials were negligible. This was why successful hunters from past eras were revered so highly.

Kasau crept forwards through the dew-soaked grass, his spear held ready. The warm, moist air filled his nose with the heady scent of the savannah as the eastern sky lightened with every passing minute. The dawn chorus was building, a blend of birdsong adding to the constant cacophony of insect and amphibian noises. They were cutting it fine. He wanted to strike before the sun peered over the horizon to prevent the dawn dragon from gaining access to her full powers. If camouflaged, the dusk dragon would be difficult to locate in the half-light, but the men had been well briefed on the telltale signs to look for.

He looked to his left. Some distance away he could just make out a shadowy figure, spear in hand, easing through the long grass. A glance to his right revealed another silhouette, more obvious this time, but making no discernible noise. The circle was tightening. In just a few more minutes the dragons would be theirs for the taking.

'Damn!' Elian swore. 'They're all around us. There's no way out. What shall we do?'

'*There's always a way out, Elian. The trick is to know where to look for it. Fang, I'm going to form a gateway right in front of you, if I can. Get ready. It will be hard for me to hold it for more than a heartbeat or two as the sun is not quite at the horizon. Are you up to a very short flight . . . ? Good . . . You know what to look for. ~'t hesitate . . . I'll follow you.*'

Hearing Ra's side of the conversation she was having with Fang was strange. Elian felt as if he were eavesdropping, yet he knew that Ra wanted him to hear her words.

'A gateway?' he asked softly. 'What sort of gateway? What's going on, Ra?'

'Would you mind letting me in on what's happening?' Kira's whisper was full of frustration.

'There's no time to explain, Elian. Hold on tight and tell Kira to do the same. You might find this a little unsettling. Ready, Fang? Go!'

Elian heard Longfang launch forwards. The first down-sweep of his great wings made a loud, distinctive whooshing noise.

'Hang on, Kira. I think this is going to be a rough ride,' he advised her.

A heartbeat later Ra leaped forwards, her explosive acceleration rocking Elian back in his saddle. He instinctively glanced over his shoulder to make sure Kira was still behind him. She was – clinging grimly to the ridge in front of her.

Elian could feel Ra's intense concentration. Adrenaline surged in his stomach. She was reaching out with her mind. Whatever she was doing was not easy. They were charging at high speed towards the easternmost hunters. The spears would start flying any heartbeat. What was she thinking of?

A straight charge would be little less than suicide.

When the gateway opened, Elian sensed it, rather than saw it. His fleeting impression was of a great rent in the fabric of reality – a ghostly grey hole of swirling nothingness. One heartbeat they were barely off the ground and fast approaching a line of enemies armed with deadly spears, the next his body and mind were wrenched in gut-twisting, brain-spinning manner. For a moment he experienced a strange feeling of weightlessness, as if he were immersed in water. The sensation was fleeting, but left him reeling with dizzy disorientation. A second contorting wrench was followed by a blast of freezing air, as they emerged high into a night sky.

'Where in hell are we?' Kira yelled above the sudden roar of the biting wind.

The question echoed the turmoil in Elian's mind, for he knew the instant the air rammed into his nostrils that they were no longer in Racafi. Aside from the massive temperature drop, the scent of it was totally different. Wherever they were it was now the dead of night, and they were high in the air – at least a couple of thousand spans up, judging by what little he could see.

It was impossible. It made no sense. How had they got here? What had Aurora done?

Chapter Eleven
A Most Unusual Dragon

Kasau saw the portal open in the air just in front of the dragons and a cry rose in his throat. Taking three swift strides, he hurled his spear with all his strength. The yell he released burned his throat as it burst from him like the roar of an angry lion. The moment the weapon left his fingers he knew he had thrown it in vain. His eyes followed its trajectory as it sailed through the air in a deadly arc, but the dragons vanished before the spear reached them. The portal closed the instant the second dragon passed through and his spear sliced through empty air. Several other spears crisscrossed harmlessly through the same space. They were gone.

Kasau sank to his knees. The rest of the circle of hunters closed in on the spot where the two dragons had disappeared and began to mill about in confusion. Kasau could not believe it. Twice he had set traps for the dawn dragon. Both times she had slipped through his grasp. No other dragon he had tracked had ever eluded him like this. The beast had made a fool of him. He had under-estimated her abilities and she had exploited his overconfidence.

'We will meet again,' he muttered to himself. 'But next time will be the last. I'll not let you get the better of me again.'

'Where are we, Ra? What is this place and how did we get here?' Elian asked the questions aloud to allow Kira the chance to follow at least one side of his conversation.

'We've travelled to another world, Elian. This is the most special of a dawn dragon's abilities. No other dragon can come here except with one of us. At dawn and dusk the boundaries between worlds weaken. At dawn, my powers are at their maximum. There is a very small window either side of that short period when I am strong enough to open a gateway and break through the barrier.'

'Another *world*? What other world?'

'The inhabitants call it Earth. We are currently flying over a country the people here call France. The people are similar in appearance to you, but this world is not

like ours. They have no dragons. They are aware of us due to a number of encounters over the centuries, but here, we are creatures of legend. They refuse to accept that we exist.'

'Earth? France? You've been here before?' he asked, unable to mask his shock.

'Yes, but I always keep my visits as short as I can. The people here are invariably hostile towards dragons and they have developed weapons unlike any we have in our world. Last time I was here I encountered a group of men carrying things they called "muskets". They looked rather like strange sticks made of metal, but they spat fire and tiny balls of metal at tremendous speed that stung my scales, leaving spots that itched for days afterwards.'

'When was this, Ra? Are we likely to meet them?'

'I doubt it – at least not the same crowd. I believe the people here live no longer than you do, and that encounter was over one hundred season rotations ago in the time of this world. I've not needed to use the gateways again until today.'

A distant sound drew Elian's attention. Irregular crumps and thumps sounded close, yet had to be coming from the ground. What could cause such a noise?

Looking down Elian noticed strange flashes of light and occasional dashed lines streaking across the countryside with impossible speed. Then flashes lit the sky nearby, red and orange fire blossoming with loud reports. The explosions were both startling and frightening, tying a twisting knot of fear in Elian's stomach.

Kira suddenly tapped Elian on the shoulder. Her face in the dark looked as scared as he felt. 'Fang says there are thousands of men fighting below us. Tens of thousands even. He doesn't know how, but they're killing each other despite being hundreds of paces apart. The entire countryside below us has been torn apart by war. Where in Areth are we?'

'That's just it – we're not in Areth any more. Ra says we've travelled to another world, Kira. She says men here have invented strange weapons that spit death over great distances.'

'I don't like it,' she said. 'Tell Ra to take us back. I'd rather take my chances with the hunters than get caught up in the mess down there.'

'Agreed. Ra, can you take us back?'

'Yes,' she replied, '*but not yet – we must wait until dawn.*'

'Dawn! But that must be hours away. We'll freeze to death. My hands and face are already numb.'

'*I know, but I can only open a gateway at dawn. Time here does not run with the same cadence as it does in* our world. Longfang and I have been discussing which side of the lines of fighting we should land.'

'What have you decided?' Elian asked, his teeth chattering.

'We haven't. He wants to land to the west. I want to let the wind carry us to the east.'

Another noise, not sharp and explosive like the other sounds they had heard, but continuous and droning, drew Elian's attention.

'What's that?' he asked aloud, not really expecting an answer. Whatever it was, impossible though it seemed, it was getting closer.

There was a pause.

'Longfang has better night-vision than I. He thinks it might be a strange form of dragon that we've never encountered before. We both tried calling out, but the dragon hasn't responded. He bears two dragonriders, but has no consciousness that we can reach. From what I sense of the thoughts of the dragonriders, they are preoccupied with getting home.'

'A dragon!' Elian was startled. 'But you said that they didn't have any dragons here.'

'It appears my information was incorrect.'

'Has he seen us?'

'I don't believe so, but it's hard to tell. I'm calling the dragon "he" for convenience, for I can sense no gender. If he is a dragon, then he's a most odd-looking fellow. His riders seem to be embedded in his back.'

As the dragon approached, so the explosions came closer as well.

'Is the dragon making those flashes? Is this another one of your dragon secrets?' Elian asked.

'I have no idea what's causing them, Elian. The dragonriders are doing their best to ignore the flash fires, but they both fear them. The impression I get is that the fire originates from the ground, though that seems unlikely.'

Elian wasn't so sure. Having seen the speed at which the lines of fire had sped through the night below them, he was not ready to discount anything at this point. Maybe this dragon was somehow involved in the fighting. Dragons in Areth didn't engage in the conflicts of men, but that did not mean the same would hold true here.

'Can we follow him, Ra? But let's stay out of sight. Maybe if we land near him, we'll get a chance to find out what's going on.'

'Very well. I shall keep Fang between the strange dragon and us. I doubt that they will penetrate his camouflage. It looks as if they have begun to descend, so we should be able to stalk him with ease.'

How long they glided along behind the droning dragon, Elian could not have said. By the time the strange-looking creature landed in a wide field,

Elian was frozen nearly as badly as he had been on his first day.

On the way down he noted that the dragon they were following, aside from making the strange droning sound, was a very strange shape. It had two sets of main wings, one above the other, which seemed to be solid and unmoving. Its wingspan was about two-thirds that of Aurora's and it had a third, smaller set of wings near its tail. The creature was also unnaturally short, measuring less than half of Aurora's length. It looked ungainly, rather like a bee – whose body size compared to its wingspan had always defied reason.

Its legs appeared thin and spindly with strange joints. They looked almost like the legs of a giant insect, but shorter, and not at all similar to the strong legs of a dragon. Perhaps it wasn't a dragon at all, but some sort of outsized insect. If so, then how had the men flying on its back tamed it?

The creature landed between two lines of fiercely burning torches. As it ran across the grass Elian noticed yet another strange thing. Its legs were not moving! Was it sliding? In what little light there was from the path of lights, he could just make out that the creature's feet were round like the wheels of a wagon, but much smaller.

'Is the dragon actually a flying wagon?' he

wondered aloud. 'That would be amazing! It makes sense too. If the people here are clever enough to make weapons that spit death over large distances, why not a flying wagon?' Elian wanted to take a closer look.

There were some very large buildings at the edge of the field, far larger than any he had ever seen in Racafi – some large enough to house several dragons at once. It stood to reason that the men would reside there. Elian directed Aurora to land a good distance away, concealed in the darkness. His teeth were chattering and his body was shaking wildly as Ra settled on the ground. When he turned, Kira was similarly suffering.

'I'm s-s-sorry, Kira,' he shivered. 'We c-can't risk a f-fire here. Get F-fang to curl up. Y-you can shelter in the h-hollow he makes. He can c-c-cover you with a w-wing. If you snuggle down with your b-b-b-blankets, you should warm up quickly.'

'W-what about you?' she stammered, her mouth struggling to form the words.

'I-I-I'd like to get a c-closer look at that d-d-dragon. Then I'll d-do the same with R-ra.'

'Don't!' she said quickly. 'W-we don't want to g-get caught here. Why d-don't you s-sleep next t-t-to me? We'd w-warm up quicker if we h-huddled together,' she suggested. 'H-hunters do it all the time.'

Elian nodded. The idea of getting a close look at the flying wagon was very appealing, but he knew she was right. It would be risky. Also, he felt so cold that snuggling together sounded like a far better idea. 'All right. If you're sure,' he said.

He slid from Ra's back. The temperature at ground level was far cooler than night-time in Racafi, but it wasn't freezing. He held out his hands and helped Kira to dismount gently. No sooner had her feet touched the ground than she shook off his hands.

'Just d-d-don't get the wrong idea,' she said abruptly and staggered away towards Fang.

'Not a ch-chance,' he replied, trying to force his frozen lips into a smile.

Elian knew Kira valued her independence, but it was interesting to see she was not above putting it aside when experience or common sense dictated. If she did not want to show weakness – that was fine by him.

'No offence, Ra, but I'm going to sleep with Kira and Fang tonight,' Elian thought, struggling to concentrate.

'I understand,' she replied. *'Sharing warmth is a*

good way of bonding. You want her to be your friend. This is a good way forwards. Sleep well, Elian.'

'What if someone finds us in the night?'

'Don't worry, Elian. I'll wake you if need be.'

'But if we need to talk with them . . .' he started. 'Will they understand Racafian?'

'No, they won't. There are many languages in this world. None would make any sense to you, but don't worry. I can help. If we have need of communication, you can speak and I'll do the translating. Just speak as you normally do. I will do my best to see that you hear the native's speech in Racafian and I will try to control your words so that the native hears your words in his native tongue.'

'You can do that? Fantastic!' Elian tried to imagine how such a process could work.

'In theory, yes. I must admit that I've never actually tried it, but I've met dragons who have. They said it was not difficult, but you must understand that the translations might not be entirely accurate, and it will take me a moment or two to establish the link.'

'How "not entirely accurate" are we talking here?'

'I'm afraid that's a question for which I have no answer,' Ra admitted.

Elian considered the possible problems that might arise as a result of misunderstandings. Having already seen some of the destructive capabilities of these people, apprehension tightened the muscles of his back and shoulders as he imagined what they could do to him if he were perceived as an enemy.

'Let's hope no one finds us, then,' he thought.

Chapter Twelve
Dragon Terror

Elian found it impossible to sleep next to Kira for long. Cuddling up close whilst they were shivering with cold was fine. It felt good and comforting, especially after seeing the strange fighting and the flash bang fires earlier. They both drifted into an uneasy sleep quite quickly. However, once he had warmed up, Elian woke up feeling uncomfortable. Kira's breathing was settled and her body had relaxed into sleep. Taking care not to wake her, he eased away and arranged all the blankets over her.

Fang was also asleep, so Elian repositioned himself within the hollow circle Fang had made and waited for morning. As dawn approached, Fang stirred and Elian climbed the dragon's side to peer out from under the cover of his wing. The increasing light revealed a lush green countryside rich with vegetation and perfect for farming. What his father would give to have land like this to cultivate! It was a farmer's paradise.

Kira appeared silently beside him. Her face betrayed nothing of her thoughts, but Elian felt more comfortable with the silence than he had the previous day.

The wait for dawn to break was a nervous one. They were all anxious to leave this strange land and return to Areth. Fang's wound needed urgent attention and every moment they stayed increased the chance of their being discovered. They saw one of the strange dragon-like things launch across the field and climb into the slowly brightening sky. To Elian's excitement he could see that his deduction had been correct. The beast was not alive, but a man-made contraption. The machine had a single rider and Elian wondered if the man would notice them as he gently circled into the sky above. The heartbeats dragged into an eternity, but finally the sun peeped over the horizon. It was time for them to move.

Elian and Kira crouched low to Ra's back as they launched. On one side a line of trees masked their take-off. On the other side Fang shielded them as much as possible with his camouflage, carefully positioning himself between Ra and the men and machines now moving around their great houses.

'*He's seen us,*' Ra announced as they accelerated. '*The one in the air is looking at us right now.*'

'Have others seen us as well?' Elian asked.

'*No. Just the flying one. No one on the ground appears to have noticed. But I can feel the surprise of the one in the air. He's debating if we are real.*'

At the crucial moment of dawn, the boundary between worlds was at its weakest and Ra was able to open a far bigger gateway than she had when they had escaped the dragonhunters. It was wide enough for the two dragons to enter side by side. They plunged into the vortex and out of the war-torn world. The mind-twisting wrench of passage, the momentary sensation of weightlessness, and the dizzying effect of emergence were just as disorienting to Elian as they had been the first time. He half expected to reappear above the same water hole in the savannah that they had left from, but the view that met his eyes was very different.

Jack reached an altitude of about five hundred feet and began a gentle turn to the left, seeking to gain as much height as practical before striking out for the enemy lines. As he climbed, he scanned the brightening sky for hostile aircraft, but the airspace above, around and below him remained clear.

It was as he was passing about six thousand feet that he noticed a strange shape in the corner of the airfield. Although the sun had peeped above the horizon up at his altitude, lighting the blue, blue sky with its bright golden rays, he could see that down on the ground dawn was still a few moments away. What *was* that long, sleek thing? If he didn't know better, he would have said it looked like a dragon.

For the first time in ages, Jack laughed aloud in the air. A *dragon!* What was he thinking? This war must be getting to him. He rubbed his goggles with the back of his glove, suspecting a smear of oil, but the goggles were clear. For a moment he returned his attention heavenwards, scanning the sky for hostile aircraft. He couldn't afford a lapse in concentration over something so ridiculous. He looked down again at the huge, bronze shape and then across to the hangar area where a number of machines were being brought out onto the field. Why didn't anyone on the ground react to its presence? Was he the only one who could see it? Truly, he prayed he wasn't going mad.

Suddenly the colour of the object changed from a bronze/brown to a resplendent gold as the sun cleared the horizon at ground level. To Jack's further amazement a grey, swirling vortex that looked somewhat like a tiny spinning disk appeared in the air not a hundred yards from the thing. The vortex was strangely two-dimensional. Jack could see it swirling, yet from directly above, or to the side, it looked invisible, without depth.

The golden thing, whatever it was, suddenly launched towards the vortex with surprising acceleration. As it ran, great wings unfolded and began to beat. A quick comparison with the aircraft being wheeled out of the hangar revealed a wingspan greater by a considerable margin than that of the aircraft below. Then it was gone; swallowed by the swirling vortex, which promptly collapsed and vanished.

Jack blinked a few times in rapid succession. There was nothing but empty space below him. His colleagues were going about their normal business. If it had been real, then surely someone on the ground would have spotted it. He would wait and see if anyone mentioned it later. If they did, then fine – he would share what he had seen. If not . . .

'Go and find some enemies to scare, Jack,' he muttered to himself under his mask. 'Talk of dragons will do no one any good.'

Elian's first breath drew in clean air, tinged with the pungent scent of pine. It was warm, but not with the tropical heat of the savannah. The air here had the feel of summer about it. They were gliding across a huge area of dense forest, which marched right to the curving shores of a large lake, and onwards again from the far shore into the distance. To the north, great mountains of purple-grey rock thrust thousands of spans into the blue sky. Bright patches of snow speckled the mountaintops with majestic white, whilst occasional puffs of fair-weather cloud and a few lenticular caps to the leeward side of the distant peaks punctuated the blue heavens. As they neared the lake, the sun set the surface of the water sparkling with dancing gold. The scenery was breathtaking.

A blurring to their right drew Elian's attention as Fang shed his camouflage and appeared alongside them.

'Where are we, Ra? This doesn't look, or smell, like Racafi.'

'I'm not surprised, Elian. We are in northern Cemaria, several thousand leagues from your home.'

'Where? Good grief, Ra! This type of travel is a neat trick, but aren't we as far from Orupee here as we were in Racafi?'

'True, but Longfang needs healing, and my dragon-sense – my instinct, if you like – opened the gateway here for us to see that need fulfilled.'

Elian considered that for a moment as they glided

down and across the lake towards the far shore. It made little sense to him.

'Isn't there a day dragon in Orupee that could have helped?' he asked. 'I thought dragons roved all over the world.'

'Most likely, but it would not have been the right day dragon,' Ra answered haughtily. 'Dragonsense is not something that can easily be explained to humans. It has to do with destiny and purpose. A dragon has a sense of "rightness" when she is following her destiny. Beware, though, for this should not be confused with safety. There are no safe paths, and not all encounters work out as a dragon might wish. A true dragon always follows dragonsense, though. If I were to do as I pleased, rather than following the purpose for which I was born, my existence would cease to have meaning and the world would be a poorer place. Time and again throughout Areth's history, it has been dragons following their dragonsense who have shaped the most pivotal moments, averting disasters and setting events in motion that have been to the benefit of all. There is nothing of chance in this. It is inbuilt. It is the greatest of the abilities we have been blessed with.'

They descended further and further until they were almost skimming the surface of the water. As they approached the narrow strand of clear ground between water and woods on the far side of the lake, Ra tilted into a turn and Elian could sense her pleasure as she deliberately trailed the tip of her left wing along the surface of the lake like a giant gull.

With admirable accuracy her turn brought her perfectly over the narrow beach area and she back-winged to a gentle landing. Fang landed just a few paces behind. The dusk dragon let out a hiss as he settled and Elian heard Kira's sharp intake of breath as she experienced echoes of her partner's pain.

'Are you all right?' he asked, turning in his saddle.

Kira nodded, but her face looked pale. Elian moved to put his hand on her shoulder, but the glare he received stopped him before he had raised his arm more than halfway.

What is it with her? he wondered. She's more prickly than a prickle-pig! Aloud, he addressed Ra, whose head had twisted round on her long neck until she could regard him closely with her huge eyes. 'So where's the day dragon, Ra?'

'*About ten paces in front of you, Elian. Do you not have eyes in that little human head of yours?*'

Elian looked ahead and realised that what he had taken for a line of blue-grey rocks was actually the head and neck of a dragon protruding from the tree line. Its body was largely hidden amongst the pines. The dragon looked nothing like he had expected. He had always imagined a day dragon to have glorious blue scales, and a proud, upstanding posture. This dragon looked tired, washed-out and grey.

'*What's the matter with it?*' he projected, looking at the dragon with a mixture of curiosity and caution. Something was not right here. There was no sign of the dragon's rider. Was it a rogue?

'He *is worried and a little depressed,*' Ra answered, her emphasis and tone clearly disapproving of Elian's use of 'it'. '*Human troubles, I believe.*' She snorted, though whether she did so in amusement or in disapproval of Elian's diction, he could not tell.

'*Dragonhunters?*' Elian asked, his eyes instinctively scanning the tree line for signs of movement and his heart accelerating at an alarming rate.

'*No, not hunters. It's his rider; she doesn't want him.*' Ra's tone was scathing.

'*Doesn't want him!*' The shock of it brushed aside Elian's momentary panic. '*I don't get it. You said we were predestined. Is this dragon's rider different?*'

'*No. The bonding leaves no choice,*' Ra said firmly. '*She is Firestorm's rider whether she likes it or not. According to him, the girl's mind is filled with a maelstrom of fear. Worse, it appears she is more terrified of him than anything else. She runs from him whenever he draws near. He is devastated. For a day dragon,*

142

courage is the most important attribute in a rider. The day dragon fraternity value their reputation for bravery above all else. A cowardly rider will make Firestorm the laughing stock of his kind.'

'Can Firestorm help Fang?' Elian asked, worried for a moment that they had come here in vain.

'*Yes, he has already agreed to do so. His depression won't prevent him from helping us. It is a matter of honour for a day dragon to assist those in need.'*

'*Excellent.'*

Elian remained close to Ra as Fang limped forwards and turned to allow Firestorm to see the wound. Kira ran to be by her dragon's side, but then paused, dithering for a moment before stepping reluctantly away to the side. Longfang looked at her and Elian felt he could almost hear their exchange as he observed the expressions on their faces. Kira was not happy to have to stand so far away, but she did as she was told.

Firestorm turned his head on his long neck until his nostrils were no more than a handspan from the gaping hole in Fang's thigh. The day dragon paused and stared intently at the wound for a heartbeat before drawing in a deep, slow breath.

'*What's he going to do?*' Elian asked.

'*He's going to breathe his fire over the wound,*' Ra replied.

'He's going to sear the wound! I could have done that last night!'

'No, Elian. Firestorm isn't going to sear it. Watch and you'll see.'

The day dragon breathed out, but the fire that he blew was no roaring orange flame. It seemed to ease from the dragon's mouth like a blue whisper of cloud, covering Fang's wound in a nimbus of hazy blue fire. At first nothing seemed to be happening, but Firestorm did not stop. His breath kept coming and coming. When finally he ceased, the blue nimbus clung to Fang's leg for a few seconds more before dispersing.

Kira ran to Fang's side the moment the fire dispersed. Elian was not far behind her. To his amazement, the wound had not just been seared shut by the fire – it had totally healed. There was no sign on Fang's thigh that he had ever been wounded at all. It was a miracle.

He watched as Kira tenderly ran her fingers over her dragon's thigh, a glorious smile of pleasure lighting her face. Fang turned his head slowly towards her and Elian backed away, embarrassed. For all he would like to have taken a closer look at the site of the healed wound, this was a private moment between dragon and rider. He did not want to intrude. 'That was incredible!' Elian projected to

Ra. *'I had no idea that a day dragon's healing fire would be so effective. Firestorm has helped us. We should try to help him in return. Where's his rider and what's her name? I think I should try talking to her.'*

Ra told him. Elian called to Kira to let her know where he was going, but she took no notice. Her focus was on Fang. He thought about trying again, but decided against it. She was unlikely to miss him for the short time he intended to be gone.

He was beginning to feel hot in his flying clothes, so he stripped off his jacket and fur-lined trousers, leaving them on a large, flat rock near to where Ra was settling to bask in the sunshine. It was plenty warm enough to enjoy the freedom of a short-sleeved tunic and lightweight trousers.

This was a beautiful day to walk by the lakeside. A variety of water birds bobbed on the wavelets of the lake, whilst still others wheeled and dived above it, squawking and crying with high-pitched voices. Higher, a pair of eagles soared in elegant silence, circling in lazy, aloof fashion on the air currents.

Fish jumped frequently, chasing the flies that skimmed and swarmed over the surface. A flash of white tails startled Elian as a small herd of deer scattered in front of him. They leaped and bounded into the nearby forest with astonishing speed.

'Some hunter I'd be,' he muttered with a smile

and a rueful shake of his head. He had been within a dozen paces of them without any awareness of their presence. Their camouflage was almost as good as Fang's against the background of the trees.

He found the girl around the next bend in the shoreline, crouched by the water's edge, washing her hands. There was a strange fervour about the way she scrubbed at her skin. She looked nervous, or frightened, at having touched something. What had she been doing to require such vigorous cleaning?

As he approached her, Elian realised she was not aware of him. He did not want to frighten her further, so he introduced himself from a few paces away.

'Hello, Nolita. I'm Elian.'

He was right to be cautious. Nolita leaped up like a startled cat, and Elian found himself facing a skinny, wild-eyed girl with a belt knife that she had drawn so fast he had not seen her hand move.

'Stay away from me! Don't come any closer. I'll use this if I have to.'

'Hey, relax! I believe you,' Elian said slowly, raising his hands to show he was unarmed. 'I've just come to see if you're all right. Your friend was worried about you.'

'My friend? I don't have any friends around here.

Who sent you? Not . . . the beast? Has it found me again? Please tell me it hasn't! It has, hasn't it? Did it talk to you as well? Why won't it leave me alone? I can't take much more of this!'

The girl's panic-filled blue eyes darted around to look for signs of Firestorm, but never left Elian for more than a heartbeat. He took in the odd contrast between her dishevelled, dirty clothing and her clean hands, face and hair. Her shoulder-length blond tresses looked recently combed. The strange mixture of care and disarray was a mystery.

When she had satisfied herself that the dragon was nowhere close by, Nolita's shoulders slumped and tears of relief formed in her eyes. Elian took a step forward with the intention of offering comfort, but with a blur of speed the girl was poised with her knife once more.

'You won't catch me that easily,' she snarled. 'What do you want?'

'I told you – I came to see if you're all right. Your friend, Firestorm, is very worried about you.'

What was it with girls? Elian wondered. Twice in two days he had tried to help them only to find himself facing a deadly length of steel. The next time he tried to help someone he resolved to keep his jacket on. At least the thick leather would offer some protection.

'You . . . you're one of . . . of them, aren't you? Don't deny it. You couldn't know the beast's name if you weren't.'

'If you mean I'm a dragonrider, then yes, I'm "one of them",' Elian responded with a nod of acknowledgement. 'I just met my dragon a few days ago. I'm here with another rider, Kira, and her dragon, Longfang. They've not been together much longer than Aurora and me. Hunters injured Fang a couple of days back. Your dragon kindly healed him.'

As he spoke, Nolita's hands began to shake and what little colour there had been in her cheeks drained away until her skin reminded Elian of the corpse of an old man who had died in the fields the previous harvest. For a moment he thought she might vomit.

'It's *NOT MINE*! I want nothing to do with it,' she spat.

She shuddered violently and with a sudden flash of insight Elian began to understand what was going on inside her head. His use of the word 'dragon' had set her hands shaking. Some feared snakes or spiders. Others feared heights or enclosed spaces. Nolita, it seemed, had an intense fear of dragons.

Elian could understand something of her terror. After all, his own first thoughts when he had met

Ra were of becoming her lunch. A dragon was a top predator – a beast worthy of fear. The only major difference between Nolita and himself was that he had accepted the evidence of the dragon's friendly behaviour where she had not. How could he help her overcome her fears and accept the truth?

'It seems you've got a problem, Nolita,' Elian said softly, taking care to keep his hands in front of his body. 'Firestorm's going to keep following you until you accept him. Partnerships between dragons and riders can't be changed. I'll be honest – I understand that Firestorm isn't thrilled about it either. I think he expected his rider to be more enthusiastic.'

'Do I look like I care what that thing thinks?' she snapped. 'I'd rather die than be near it.'

'Try not to be so negative,' Elian continued, keeping his voice calm and reasonable. 'It's a great honour to be a dragonrider. Some people spend their whole lives dreaming of what it would be like to be chosen.'

'I don't want honour. I just want to be left alone. I don't want any of those creatures anywhere near me. Make it go away. You're a rider. Get your beast to tell it. It won't listen to me.'

'No, of course he won't!' Elian said, shaking his head. 'He wouldn't listen to Aurora either. He can't. Don't you see? Neither of you has any choice in this. Destiny can't be altered. If it could, then dragons could pick and choose their riders. You're afraid. So was I when I met Ra. In fact I was so scared that I accidentally backed off a cliff. Only Ra's quick thinking saved me from being a splatter of mush in the Haleen Valley.'

'You fell? Off a cliff?' she asked, her voice cracking with amazement. 'Are you mad? You wouldn't catch me anywhere so high. I can't even climb a tree without getting dizzy. If I go anywhere high up my stomach churns until I puke.'

Inwardly Elian groaned. It was getting worse and worse. If that was her reaction to heights, then it was a fair bet that she would be terrified of flying. How could he hope to help her? Her fears were so deeply rooted. It was time to return to Ra and admit defeat.

Chapter Thirteen
Facing the Fears

'*We're not leaving without Firestorm and Nolita,*' Ra told Elian, her mental voice strong with determination. '*Fang feels it too. We're meant to help these two resolve their problems so they can come with us to see the Oracle.*'

'Then I hope you like the scenery here, Ra, because we're going to be in this spot for a very long time. Nolita's terrified of dragons. The only way you'd get her on Firestorm's back would be to knock her out and tie her there! If we were in Racafi I could make a potion to help calm her fears, but I don't recognise the herbs and plants here. If I tried to make something, I might accidentally poison her. I daren't risk it.'

Ra's nostrils flared. She snorted in a most unlady-like fashion and then lowered her head until her lower jaw rested on a large, flat rock in front of Elian. Her huge eyes of amber stared through him in such a way that for a moment he wondered if she were looking into another dimension.

'Sounds like you're going to need my help again.'

Elian jumped. He hadn't heard Kira approach. A twinkle in Aurora's eyes gave Elian the impression that she had enjoyed seeing Kira catch him unawares. He clenched his teeth beneath tightened lips and schooled his expression as he turned to face his fellow rider. Much as he felt his bond with Ra was growing stronger every day, he did find her sense of humour irritating at times.

Kira had changed out of her flying gear and was now wearing a brown tunic, several lengths of colourful beads around her neck, and a short skirt.

'Do *you* get scared then, Kira?' he asked. 'You don't seem the type.'

'No. Not much frightens me,' she admitted as she sat down cross-legged on the ground next to him. 'But there was a boy in my tribe who was a bit like Nolita.' She grinned, her teeth gleaming white and her dark eyes sparkling with amusement.

'And?' he prompted. Despite his annoyance at having been startled, Elian was intrigued.

Kira bent and picked up a stick with which she started drawing patterns idly in the mud.

'The boy was terrified of snakes. Just the mention of a snake would make him run a mile. The men were really embarrassed to see the boy acting so cowardly. Our Medicine Man said his only hope was to face more and more snakes until he learned to control his fear.'

'Did it work?' he asked.

'It went quite well until the boy chose the wrong snake to stand and face.' Kira looked up from her doodling and met his gaze. 'It bit him.'

'Ouch! I'll bet that made it even harder for him the next time,' Elian said, wincing.

'Actually there wasn't any next time,' she replied nonchalantly, returning to her scribbles. 'The snake was poisonous. The boy died within minutes.'

Elian's jaw dropped. 'Great!' he exclaimed, shaking his head in disbelief. 'Can I suggest you don't mention that story to Nolita? I don't think she'd appreciate the ending.'

Kira's grin stretched wider and she cocked her head slightly as she viewed the marks she had made. 'The principle of the Medicine Man's cure was good, though. And at least in Nolita's case there's no chance of her dragon biting her.'

'True,' he admitted. 'But as we've already

seen, riding a dragon can be dangerous in other ways. How do you suggest we convince her to face Firestorm, let alone ride him?'

'I guess we're just going to have to lead her by the hand.'

'That might not be as easy as you think,' Elian said with a sigh. 'You haven't met Nolita.'

Kira looked up and casually discarded the stick. 'Then it's time I did,' she said, standing up and brushing down the back of her skirt. She drew one foot across the patterns she had drawn, destroying them with a single sweep. 'Beautiful as this place is, I don't want to get stuck here. Now that Fang's healed, he's itching to get to the Oracle. His itch is already annoying me nearly as much as it is him, but he's convinced we should stay and help Firestorm.'

Elian knew what she meant. As his bond with Aurora was deepening, he found he was sensing more and more of her feelings. Her conviction that it was right to stay and help Firestorm was firm, but he wondered how long it would be before the draw of the Oracle would prove too strong to ignore.

'Come on then. We'd better get moving.' Kira picked up her knapsack and looped it over her shoulder. The two walked along the water's edge until they rounded the corner where Elian had last seen Nolita. He scanned the line of the trees, but there were no signs of her anywhere.

'This was where I spoke with her, but it looks like she's on the run again.'

'I wouldn't be so sure,' Kira said softly. 'Nolita's not far away. She's watching us.'

'Where?'

'Don't keep looking round, you fool!' she hissed, picking up a smooth, flat pebble and sending it skimming across the surface of the water. 'I trained as a hunter for my tribe, remember? I can read the signs. She's in the trees.' She paused for a moment and then continued. 'Let's see if we can draw her out. Start gathering up some of this driftwood. I'm going to make a fire.'

'Here? By the water?'

'Yes,' Kira affirmed. 'Here. Just do as I say. It's a nice spot for a picnic. I think it's time we had breakfast. Nolita must be hungry too. The breeze is in the right direction. If I was going to put coin on what would bring her into the open, then I reckon the smell of cooking meat would be a fair bet.'

Elian paused for a moment, looking for flaws in Kira's plan, but as he had no better ideas he decided not to criticise.

There was plenty of driftwood along the shore-line. Kira sorted the wood and placed the smaller sticks carefully into a cone shape before taking some dry tinder from her pack and tucking it into a recess in the centre of the stack. A few strikes of her flint and steel sent showers of sparks into the tinder. Within moments Kira was nursing a tiny flame, which licked hungrily and spread through the sticks. When she was sure it was not going to die, she started to add progressively larger pieces of wood, feeding the fire in a way that encouraged its orange tongues to grow until it reached the optimum size for cooking.

From her knapsack, she took a small cooking pan and several strips of venison wrapped in leaf bundles. From the strip of fat she had saved from the carcass of the deer, she cut a small piece and wiped it around the pan to grease the surface. The remainder she left in the pan to add flavour.

Digging deeper into her pack, she found her wraps of herbs, from which she carefully chose a couple of sprigs and proceeded to strip them with her fingers, dropping the leaves into the greasy pan. When she was satisfied that she had enough, she placed the remainder to one side, added strips of meat to the pan and then held it over the flames. Within a few heartbeats, the contents began to sizzle gently. A wonderful aroma began to exude from the pan and Elian's stomach began to rumble.

Although it looked to be nearly midday here they had not yet eaten, and the smell of frying meat set his mouth watering.

'That smells fantastic!' he said, taking care to keep the fire between them.

'That's the general idea. We'll probably have to eat some to draw Nolita out. I'm guessing you won't object to that part of the plan.' She grinned across the fire at him.

'I think I'll live with it,' he responded.

'Right, why don't you go and collect a few nuts from the edge of the woods? They'll go well with the meat. Our friend will come into the open soon enough.'

Elian wanted to retort that as Kira was the trained hunter, it should be her job to risk meeting the pointed end of Nolita's knife. It also occurred to him that it was probably too early in the season to find nuts, but he did not want to blurt out his suspicion in case it highlighted his ignorance of seasonal differences between Racafi and Cemaria. Rather than look cowardly, or a fool, he held his tongue.

He walked across to the edge of the forest and began searching the fringe for nuts. He foraged for a while, but the only pine nuts he found were not yet ripe enough to eat. It felt good to be right.

'Stand still! Don't move unless you want me to stab you.' Nolita's order came from directly behind him.

All good feelings vanished. The touch of Nolita's knifepoint in the small of his back sent chills running up and down his body.

Damn! he thought. How is it that everyone can move silently through woodland except me? He raised his hands slowly to show that he did not intend to put up a fight.

'*You don't listen properly,*' Ra announced in his mind, her tone amused. '*I heard her through your ears. Don't worry. She doesn't intend to hurt you.*'

'Turn around,' Nolita ordered. 'Come on! Don't take all day about it. Keep your hands where I can see them. Now, we're going to visit your friend out there by the water and you're going to give me some of that food you're cooking.'

'There's no need for threats, Nolita,' he replied, keeping his voice calm and unthreatening. 'We're cooking plenty for you as well. All you had to do was ask.'

Nolita watched as Elian came closer, foraging through the brush and checking the branches of the pines. It was too early for pine nuts. Did the boy know nothing?

Silent as a fox, she slipped out from behind the large tree and crept up behind him. Determination welled inside her as she pressed the point of her knife gently against Elian's back. He looked more irritated than afraid when she told him to turn round. He had not heard her coming. She would wager everything she owned on it. So why did he react with such nonchalance when she appeared behind him with a knife? It made little sense.

She had fought with her hunger for days as she had run from the beast. The beast's voice in her head had made her wonder if she was insane. It had teased her with offers of food. It had feigned concern, but she had realised from the outset that this was a trick. Somehow the beast had insinuated its thoughts into her mind, but she had fought it at every turn. Now, her belly knotted and cramped at the prospect of a proper meal.

Elian was a rider. He had said so. But none of the beasts were in sight. This was a gamble. If Elian was seeking to trap her, then she would have to risk it.

Desperation warred with her fears. She could feel her strength failing. She had to eat soon, or the forest would likely claim her. 'Better the forest than ... she cut off the thought and concentrated on keeping her knife hand steady. No. This will work. The riders have food. I'll take what I need and disappear back into the forest before the beast realises what's happening.

'Lead the way, Elian,' she ordered. 'Keep your hands where I can see them. Don't try anything. I don't want any trouble. I just want to eat.'

'Fair enough, Nolita.'

His voice sounded calm. How could he stay so collected when he must be terrified inside? Her brother and sister were brave like Elian. A spark of envy flashed through her, but she snuffed it out in an instant. Her fear had kept her alive. She needed it. It made her strong in ways other people didn't understand.

They moved swiftly out across the strand to where Kira was busy cooking. As they approached, Nolita gave a sudden gasp of shock.

'What's the matter, Nolita? Are you all right?'

Nolita did not answer. She was staring with rigid fascination at Kira's face. Kira looked up from her cooking with a big, friendly smile.

'Hello, Nolita. I've been expecting you. Sit down and have some food. It's just about cooked.'

'Your face! What happened to your face?' Nolita asked, her eyes wide with shock as she looked at Kira with open horror.

'My face? Oh, my tribal marks, you mean?

They're painted ... no, that's not it, is it? Do you mean the colour of my skin?'

'The elders in my village tell tales of demons with black skin,' Nolita admitted, as if not sure whether to be terrified, or embarrassed.

To Nolita's astonishment, rather than take offence at her admission the dark girl laughed at her.

'Well, there might be a few lads from my tribe who would describe me as a demon after I'd tossed them out of a wrestling circle.' Kira chuckled. 'But I can assure you they'd be exaggerating. The tribal people of Racafi outnumber the light-skins by around seven to one. Elian can tell you, if you don't believe me. Come − sit. The meat is perfect. It would be a shame to let it go cold. Go ahead. Use your knife and take some.'

'You − Elian. Eat some first,' Nolita ordered, eyeing the food suspiciously.

One of Kira's eyebrows rose sharply in an amused, quizzical fashion, but she said nothing. Elian was more than happy to oblige. He took a piece of meat from the pan and began eating it enthusiastically.

'Swallow,' Nolita ordered.

Elian did so and then took another bite from the meat in his hand. 'Mmm! Very tasty, Kira!' he mumbled through a large mouthful. 'You should cook more often.'

Nolita waited a moment or two longer, watching Elian intently for any signs of immediate illness. He looked fine, so she nodded to Kira and speared a piece of meat with her knife. At the first bite, her eyes widened. Elian was right; the meat was succulent and bursting with rich flavour.

'Take a seat. There's no rush and we have plenty. I can always cook more if you like,' Kira offered, indicating a flat rock on the other side of the fire. 'We heard you were having problems with a dragon. Would you like to talk about it? We might be able to help.'

Nolita flinched at the word 'dragon'. Her heart started beating faster and her eyes darted around nervously. There were no signs of the beast, but that did not stop her from double checking. It took a moment or two for the feelings to subside enough for her to talk.

'No, I'd rather not, if you don't mind,' she replied. 'The meat is very good. Thank you. It's been a while since I ate good meat.'

'It's your choice, of course,' Kira said casually, reaching into her pack.

Nolita raised her knife hand automatically as her suspicion flared, but when Kira drew out another large piece of meat it was hard for Nolita to hide her delight. She visibly relaxed. Kira had emptied the contents of the pan into a small bowl for her, and it was disappearing fast. Seeing Kira preparing more set her stomach rumbling.

'How long would you give her after we're gone?' Kira asked, speaking to Elian as if Nolita was not within a hundred leagues.

Elian looked thoughtful for a moment. 'A week,' he replied. 'Maybe two now that you've fed her.'

'We could help her,' Kira observed. 'It's probably our duty to now that we're dragonriders.'

Is this a trick, after all? Nolita wondered, turning her head to see how Elian would respond to the girl's comment. Have I walked into a trap?

'You're probably right,' Elian said.

The girl is running the show, Nolita concluded. Elian's just following her lead.

A sudden whoosh of air brought Nolita to her feet. She spun, her knife at the ready. Panic ripped through her and her vision momentarily blurred as she fought back the instinct to faint. Two beasts, the blue coloured one that had been following her and another with scales of glowing gold, had approached silently over the treetops. Vast wings, fearsome horns and terrifying scaly bodies seemed to fill the sky. They were landing one to either side of the fire. Her only hope was the cover of the trees.

Without a second thought, she dropped the bowl of meat and set off at a sprint. It was not far to the trees. The beasts were still trying to land, their wings stirring the air into spinning vortices in their efforts to kill their forward momentum and settle on the narrow strand. She still had a chance. If she could reach the trees before they caught her, she might yet escape.

Keeping her eyes focused on the nearest entry point to the forest, she ran as she had never run before. For a moment it seemed as if she would make it, but in one terrifying blink of an eye everything changed. Impossibly, a third dragon materialised, as if the Creator had pointed a finger at the air in front of her and willed it to be. To her horror it was so close she could not stop and she ran into the beast's side. The impact did not hurt, but the touch of the scales against her hands and the side of her face was too much. Revulsion swept through her and a wave of merciful darkness enveloped her as she fainted.

Elian was nearly as surprised as Nolita at the sudden arrival of Ra and Firestorm. He watched the terrified girl run like the wind across the strand only to find the door to her escape route cruelly slammed shut in her face. Fang's appearance was a

164

spectacular twist to Kira's trap. To begin with Elian was too angry for words, but when he did finally speak to Kira, he did so with quiet venom in his voice.

'I suppose you think that was clever!' he hissed. 'You do realise Nolita's never going to trust us again. Why didn't you tell me what you were planning?'

Kira looked him calmly in the eye and continued to fry another piece of meat over the fire. 'Do you want me to answer, or would you like to shout at me first? I normally find that if I get the anger out of my system, I listen better afterwards.'

Elian nearly choked. He wanted to rant and shout and stamp his feet, but he could see that Kira was ready to sit there and smile sweetly at him as he did it. He would look the fool. The desire to react was almost irresistible, but somehow he held his temper under control.

'*Calm down, Elian. Kira did it this way for a very good reason,*' Ra said, her tone very matter-of-fact.

'*You! You go behind my back and you tell me to calm down,*' he steamed, glad that he was able to do so silently. '*Never mind Nolita not trusting us — how am I supposed to trust you? I thought we were a team. Why are you siding with Kira? Where's your sense of loyalty?*'

'*Don't take this the wrong way, Elian,*' Ra

responded, her voice calm and aloof, '*but a good partnership involves playing to one another's strengths. I knew from the moment Longfang relayed this plan to me that you wouldn't like it.*'

'*Damned right I don't!*'

'*You would have preferred to earn Nolita's trust and then attempt to show her that we dragons are not the beasts she thinks us to be.*'

'*And the problem with that is?*' he asked.

'*It wouldn't have worked,*' Ra replied sadly. '*Even if it had, it would have taken months, if not years, to achieve. We don't have the luxury of that sort of timescale. We must get to the Oracle. There is no time to waste on niceties.*'

'*So frightening the poor girl half to death is all right, then,*' Elian stormed, his words fired with all the force he could muster. '*Sorry, but I don't see what you've achieved.*'

'*She is afraid because she's not airborne yet,*' Ra said calmly.

'*What? You can't be serious!*' Elian exclaimed, his mind racing. '*She'd jump.*'

'*Which is why she is going to fly with you on my back to begin with, and you are going to tie her to your saddle to make sure she doesn't.*'

Chapter Fourteen
The Fight

Tying Nolita onto Elian's saddle was no easy task. The poor girl had spent a most uncomfortable night, much as Elian had in the dragonhunters' camp. She came to as they were tying her up and struggled fiercely until Kira quieted her by threatening her with a knife. They did not make Nolita's bonds quite as painfully tight as Elian's had been, but they took every precaution to stop her escaping.

As soon as she realised what Elian and Kira intended to do, and despite having her hands tied behind her back, she fought like a wildcat – kicking, biting and spitting the entire time. It was only Ra's intervention that made it possible to get her into the saddle. Twisting her head around on her long neck, Ra gave Nolita a close-up view of her impressive rows of teeth. Two heartbeats later she had passed out again.

'Thanks, Ra,' Elian grunted gratefully, heaving the girl's limp body up and into position.

'*You're going to have to hurry, Elian. We don't have a lot of time until dawn. We only have a very narrow window of opportunity.*'

'I know, I know! Kira, give me a hand here, please? Ra's chivvying me up, but I can't do this on my own. Here – I'll hold her and you tie her in position.'

Kira did the best she could. The result was not very elegant, but Elian doubted he could have done any better. Kira looked at her handiwork and shook her head.

'You're going to have trouble if she starts to panic,' she said doubtfully. 'Are you going to be all right with her like this?'

'I don't exactly have a lot of choice, do I? It's almost dawn. Ra tells me there's no time for my softly softly approach. We've got to go, so let's get it over with.'

'Good luck,' she said simply.

Elian watched her as she made her way across to Fang and climbed up onto his back. Kira was still an enigma to him. Her parting words had sounded as genuine as any he had heard her say since they had met, but he still felt she had little regard for his opinion or his abilities. What would it take for him to gain her respect?

Nolita stirred in front of him. Elian put his arms around her and pulled her into a sitting position. Aurora's leaping run forwards snapped Nolita awake in an instant. Her first reaction was to scream and struggle to break Elian's hold.

'Don't be a fool!' he yelled in her ear as Ra continued to accelerate. 'If you fall, you'll spend the flight dangling upside down. You're tied on. I'm not. If I feel us slipping, I'm going to let you fall so I can hold on. Is that what you want?'

Nolita tensed in his arms. She stopped writhing, but continued to scream. Every fibre of her body felt taut to breaking point as they launched into the air. He did not have to hear the terror in her screams to feel her panic and fear. The emotions were projecting from her like an aura. He also felt the moment when Nolita first saw the gateway. He thought it impossible for her to stiffen any further, but she did. He could not see her face, but he could imagine her wide eyes at the sight of the swirling vortex hanging over the middle of the lake.

As they entered the vortex, the overload of emotion was too much for Nolita. She went limp again. This was just as well, as the twisting wrench of emergence was followed instantly by a blast of the coldest air Elian had yet experienced. Nolita was not dressed for extreme cold. They would have to descend quickly, or she would die of exposure.

It was full daylight here.

'Why have we emerged so high?' Elian called aloud as he looked down in astonishment at the vast drop beneath them. The air felt thin and he could tell that his breathing rate had instinctively increased.

'*I don't know,*' Ra replied. She sounded puzzled. '*I followed my dragonsense. This is where it brought us. There must be a reason . . . wait a heartbeat – look out!*'

'What? Why?'

A sudden staccato stuttering noise was followed by the droning whine of one of the strange flying machines. It was not alone. Three more of the contraptions scattered around the dragons, manoeuvring hard to avoid a collision.

'*Ow!*' Ra exclaimed. '*Whatever they're spitting from those machines hurts a lot more than the muskets did. We had better get away from here fast. If one of those things hits you or the girls, it won't be pleasant.*'

Elian felt the stinging impacts through the link with Ra and winced. Ra did not appear to be hurt badly, but the sensation was uncomfortable. He craned his neck around to see where the hostile machines had gone.

'*Another one!*'

Elian instinctively ducked as another machine roared past just above their heads, but there was no spitting of weapons this time – at least not in their direction. The newcomer seemed to be chasing the other machines. He's either incredibly brave, or very stupid, Elian thought. He watched, fascinated, a strange sense of horror creeping over him as the late arrival ignored the four-to-one odds and began to spit fire and death at one of the other strange-looking contraptions.

Jack gritted his teeth and jutted out his chin. Without any thought for the odds he eased his aircraft into a dive, aiming it like a bowling ball at a rack of skittles.

As his aircraft picked up speed, so the wind began to sing in the wires. Down, down, down he went, plunging towards the enemy formation like a sparrowhawk diving at its prey. The four German Albatrosses were firmly in his sights and closing fast . . . then it happened. One moment the aircraft were in formation, the next they were scattering as three huge shapes materialised from nowhere.

Jack swore, wrenching the yoke to the left. 'What the . . .?'

There was no denying it this time. The shapes

were unmistakably dragons. But where had they appeared from and what were they doing here? He watched in fascination as the leader of the enemy formation opened fire on a gold-coloured dragon in the lead of the 'V' formation of creatures. It was probably an instinctive reaction, Jack realised. Given the same situation, his first thought would have been to pull the trigger as well, but he was still some distance away and therefore had more thinking time. He saw the enemy aircraft's tracer rounds find their target, but to his amazement the creature seemed unaffected.

The grey beast to the golden one's right vanished again. It was uncanny. One second it was there, the next it was gone. Jack did not want to think about how it had disappeared. It defied logic.

He was almost on top of the mess of aircraft and flying creatures by now. The dragons had split up the formation for him. Twisting and turning through the mêlée, he adjusted his course to keep the leader's aircraft in sight, deliberately diving behind and underneath him. Easing out of his rapid descent he zoomed back up again, closing the distance rapidly until he was no more than thirty feet beneath the tail of the lead adversary's aircraft.

For a moment he felt sorry for the enemy pilot. The man was blind to the danger approaching. Jack's tactics gave his opponent little chance at this point, but he consoled himself that this was what war was all about. Angling his machine gun upwards as far as the mounting would allow, he opened fire. At the same time he pitched his aircraft gently up and down in a quick series of oscillations. It felt rather like driving a motor car at speed along a road with a succession of gentle bumps – uncomfortable, but the effect was to spray multiple lines of bullets along the length of the underside of the enemy machine.

One long burst and Jack knew instinctively that he had added another victory to his growing tally. He turned hard to the left as the stricken aircraft rolled, a plume of black smoke trailing from the engine as it entered a dive from which there would be no recovery. But Jack had no sooner entered a turn than an incoming line of bullets tore through his own wings . . .

The enemy formation had split, but had not run far. A quick glance around revealed two of the three remaining aircraft attacking from different directions. The third aircraft was not in sight. Maybe it's gone after the dragons, he thought. Never thought I'd be saying *that* to myself! He almost chuckled aloud, then there was another rattle of gunfire, this time from beneath him. A wire pinged loose, thrashing in the airflow as more bullets clattered through his machine. He had been wrong. The third enemy pilot had not followed the dragons. He was looking to turn the tables and catch Jack at his own game.

Where are the dragons now? he wondered. He had lost sight of them. But he had enough problems already, what with three foes, all determined to avenge their leader; and a host of bullet holes through his wings.

He reversed his turn, rolling hard and pulling his aircraft around to the right. One of his opponents was thrown temporarily out of position, as he found himself forced to avoid a collision with his wingman. Another reversal, and Jack managed to fire a short burst at one of the enemy aircraft. He missed, but he was heartened to know that even though his enemies held the advantage in both numbers and position, he was still able to show his teeth.

None of the aircraft could maintain their height above the ground whilst making turns at high angles of bank. They were all losing altitude fast, but they were still many thousands of feet above the lines. The fight was becoming rather more ugly than he had anticipated. Without another quick kill, his chances of survival were low.

Minutes passed in a blur that might equally have

been an eternity. Jack fought with cool guile, yet his blood burned with the fiery heat that only a fierce, sustained rush of adrenaline could bring. Time and again he outmanoeuvred one of his opponents and gained a killing position, only to be forced to break off his attack as bullets struck his machine from another quarter.

Thousands of feet had been lost during the ferocious, wheeling fight and the ground was looming large and green beneath him. Throughout the battle he never lost track of his position. The prevailing wind was doing its best to force him over the lines, but he had worked doggedly to ensure he remained over friendly ground. It was good that he had, for, with no warning, his gun jammed mid-burst. With no weapon, and his aircraft peppered with bullet holes, his only chance of survival was to run and land as soon as he could. A cloud loomed to his left and he turned towards it, weaving as he went. A glance over his shoulder and he realised that all three enemy aircraft were hot on his tail. Too late, he saw that the cloud was not substantial enough to offer him a means of escape.

The rattle of multiple guns from behind decided it. With gritted teeth, he hauled his little scout aircraft into a gut wrenching turn to the right. If he was going down, he was determined to take one of them with him.

'They could kill him at any heartbeat, Ra,' Elian projected, his heart thumping as he watched Jack's fight from above. 'He stopped them from attacking us again. We've got to help him.'

'No!' Ra responded immediately. 'We should not interfere with the events in this world unless we absolutely have to. You don't know for certain he was doing it to help us. He might have intended to attack them regardless of our appearance. We need to land somewhere in secret. We cannot have large numbers of people here knowing of our existence.'

'Why not?' he asked. 'Your dragonsense brought us here. I thought dragonsense led you everywhere for a reason. Why would it bring us here just to run and hide? That makes no sense.'

'Dragonsense is not specific,' Ra explained. 'We are meant to be here, but what we should do whilst we are here is not so clear.'

'If you're worried about people seeing dragons, there's at least four in those flying machines who've already had a good look at us. Don't you think they'll tell others?' Elian argued, determined to make his point.

'Dragons should only fight for a just cause. We cannot be certain who is in the right here – if either side

176

is,' Ra replied, dodging the question. '*He picked this fight. He must finish it.*'

Elian watched, barely able to breathe, as the four aircraft circled, dived and weaved their intricate aerial ballet beneath him. The fight was not going well for the lone flier. He controlled his machine with great skill, frustrating his opponents time and again with his clever manoeuvres. Slowly, but surely, however, they were gaining the upper hand.

'Look into his mind, Ra,' Elian shouted suddenly, unable to watch any more without doing something. 'Tell me what you see.'

'*Oh, very well,*' she said, her tone resigned. '*If it will make you feel better.*' There was a pause. '*Strange . . .*' she said thoughtfully.

'What?'

'*It's the same man who saw us last time we were here. There's something about a familiar mind that makes it instantly recognisable.*' She paused again as she considered the implications of this discovery.

'Didn't you say that dragonsense led dragons to pivotal moments in history, Ra? What if this is one of those pivotal moments? We can't ignore it. It's too much of a coincidence.'

'*Perhaps you're right, Elian,*' she admitted. '*Perhaps we are meant to help him after all.*'

'Well, whatever we're going to do, we need to do

it *now*,' Elian urged. 'They could kill him in a heart-beat.'

'*Very well. Hold on tight. I'll co-ordinate the others.*'

Holding on to Nolita suddenly became a major challenge as Ra folded her wings and entered a steep dive. The wind tore at them with bitter claws as they accelerated. Elian's mind flashed back to his fall from the Devil's Finger. We must be approaching a similar speed, he thought. With his arms wrapped around Nolita's waist, he hung on with all his might.

Firestorm dived with them, and to his other side Elian could just make out Kira plunging on a parallel course. They were not diving directly at the circling fight, but appeared to be positioning a cloud between them and the wheeling machines. Gradually extending her wings again, Ra began to pitch out of the dive. Elian's muscles screamed as Nolita's weight seemed to increase and the force acting on his own body pressed him hard against Ra's back.

As they reached level flight the pressure suddenly reduced, but Elian did not have time to feel relief before they plunged into a wall of freezing white moisture. Needles of cold stabbed his face and, as they burst free from the cloud, he realised he had been holding his breath.

The man whom they had come to help had

banked his machine into a tight turn towards his enemies in what looked a suicidal manoeuvre. As a result his machine was belly up to the approaching dragons, leaving him blind to their approach.

Ra dipped beneath the friendly aircraft before bumping back up to fly head to head with the three hostile machines. The disconcerting rattle of weapons began again and Elian heard slivers of death whizz past him in a deadly stream. He felt more stabs of pain through his link with Ra as some of the enemy weapons struck Ra on her chest, neck and wings.

They were closing fast on the enemy. He crouched as low to Ra's back as Nolita's unconscious body allowed. Suddenly Ra seemed to bounce and there was a terrifying crunch. It was all Elian could do to hold Nolita in place. He heard the roar of Firestorm's flaming breath and felt a momentary flash of heat – then it was over. Ra's normal, rhythmic wingbeat began again and Elian sat up, heart beating wildly, as they entered a gentle turn. Looking down and back, he saw the fragmented remains of two machines tumbling through the air below, with a third spinning out of control trailing fire and black smoke. Ra and Fang had literally ripped two of the machines apart, while Firestorm had torched the third.

A sudden feeling of responsibility swept over him. Ra and the other dragons had destroyed the machines at his request. Suddenly he wondered about the men who had flown them. They were now either dead or falling to their deaths because of his decision. It was a sobering thought. If he had not been so sure he had made the right decision, it would have been easy to feel guilty.

'Did you notice, Ra?' Elian observed aloud. 'All the machines we destroyed had black crosses on their wings. The other aircraft has coloured circles. Look.'

'*You're right. I hadn't noticed that.*'

'There he goes. Look, he's waving,' Elian called out excitedly.

And he was. Waggling his wings in a rocking motion, the man flew his machine past them, waving as he went.

'*I wonder what he'll tell his colleagues when he gets down on the ground!*' Ra chuckled. '*Whatever he tells them, they are unlikely to believe him. Let's get well away from here. I think we've done quite enough interfering for one day.*'

COMBATS IN THE AIR

Squadron: 60.   Date: 24 09 16.

Type and No. of
  Aeroplane: Nieuport A215.   Time: 11.15 a.m.

Armament: Vickers.   Duty: Spl Mission.

Pilot: Capt. J. Miller MC.   Height: 15,000ft.

Observer: None.

Location: Nr Arras.

Remarks on Hostile Machine –
Type Armament, Speed, etc.

Albatross C.

—— Narrative ——

Left aerodrome at 10.30 a.m. and at 11.15
engaged 4 Albatross C.'s at 15,000ft. As I
engaged from above, saw 3 aircraft of
unknown configuration appear in front of
the enemy formation. Estimate the unknown
aircraft were twice as long as an
Albatross, with wingspan of approx 50ft.
The unknown monoplanes had been
constructed to look like dragons, complete
with flapping wings. Saw the lead enemy

aircraft fire long burst at lead unknown
with no visible damage. I followed the
lead E.A. past unknowns and fired approx.
100 rounds into the underside of his
fuselage from a range of 50ft. E.A. burst
into flames and entered a spiral dive.

Remaining 3 E.A. retaliated in a
coordinated attack. Fight continued from
15,000ft down to 6,000ft. Vickers jammed
whilst still engaged with all 3 E.A.
Dragon-configured aeroplanes reappeared,
destroying all 3 E.A. in vicinity of
Arras. Two destroyed by ramming, the third
by unknown flame-throwing weapon. Returned
12.20.

4 E.A. destroyed confirmed by A.A.

J. Miller

J. Miller

26/09/16

War Office,
Whitehall,
S.W.

Hugo

*Please see the attached combat report. Four E.A.
were confirmed destroyed by ground companies near
Arras, but Captain Miller has only claimed one
for himself.*

Capt. Miller's claims of 'dragon-like' machines with flapping wings have been discounted as unfeasible and ridiculous. His C.O. believes he is suffering hallucinations due to combat stress and has sent him home on two weeks' leave of absence.

No other allied pilots have claimed kills in the vicinity of the downed fighters. Any thoughts?

Maurice

Lieutenant General Maurice Tremelayne

27/09/16

War Office,
Whitehall,
S.W.

Maurice

Re. your memo. 26/09/16 about Capt. Miller. Quite right. He's clearly delusional. Leave of absence looks to be a sensible remedy. Suggest you send a note to his C.O. Advise him not to send Miller on solo missions for a few weeks following his return to duty.

Hugo

Field Marshal Hugo Fitzpatrick

Chapter Fifteen

Questions and Some Unexpected Answers

If anyone saw the two visible dragons make their dive from the base of the clouds to settle at the edge of the woodland glade, they did not come to investigate further. Once on the ground, the dragons moved beneath the cover of the trees. By the time Elian had managed to untie Nolita, Kira had dismounted and was there to help him lift her down out of the saddle.

'She's frozen,' he said anxiously. 'What should we do?'

'*Firestorm will revive her,*' Ra assured him, simultaneously relaying the thought through Fang to Kira. '*Place her on the ground and stand back. If Nolita has any sense, she will learn from this experience that there are great benefits to being the rider of a day dragon.*'

He is a gentle soul. She should gain some sense of that through his healing breath.'

The two young dragonriders laid Nolita gently down and stepped well clear. Firestorm moved forwards, his cornflower-blue scales seeming out of place amongst the trees. He stretched his head forwards on his long neck until his nostrils were almost touching the fabric of Nolita's jacket.

'He's not going to set fire to the forest, is he?' Elian whispered to Kira, his eyes never leaving the blue dragon.

'No. Fang tells me the healing fire isn't like a normal flame,' she replied, her voice low and full of anticipation.

Firestorm blinked a couple of times and then his eyes half-lidded. His mouth opened wide. The day dragon could have consumed the young girl in a couple of swift mouthfuls, and any bystander could have been forgiven for thinking this to be his intention. Instead, the dragon inhaled a long, deep breath, and then with infinite care he breathed out his healing nimbus of fire that enveloped Nolita's body in a writhing sheet of blue flames . . .

Time seemed to slow as Firestorm exhaled his long, healing balm of fire. Then he raised his head and stepped back to give Nolita some space. Elian shook himself as if he had just woken from a standing sleep. How long had they stood and watched Firestorm breathe his fire across the slumbering girl? One minute? Two? Longer? He could not say. Witnessing the day dragon use his healing power felt magical, although he knew magic had no part in the dragon's abilities.

Nolita stirred. Elian and Kira ran forwards to help her to sit up. Her hands felt warm to the touch. Her skin looked healthy, if slightly flushed. As she made the final transition to full consciousness her face displayed a rainbow of emotions from happy contentment through surprise into horror and disgust, before finally settling with one of confusion.

'Where am I?' she asked, looking around with frightened eyes. 'What did you do to me? I feel different.'

'All good questions,' Kira answered, flashing her white teeth in a wide smile of encouragement. 'Unfortunately none of them have easy answers. Just rest a while.'

With Nolita recovering, Elian was quick to attend to Ra. The weapons of the machines had pummelled her chest in particular. Anxious to see that she was not bleeding badly he raced around to look.

'*Don't fuss. I'll be fine, Elian,*' she assured him.

'*The weapons did not penetrate my scales. They did sting, though.*'

'*I know,*' he replied. '*I felt them.*' When he looked he could see spots of red through the golden surface of her scales. '*Can Firestorm heal these?*' he asked.

'*He can and he will,*' she answered. '*If you will move aside, he will do it now.*'

Elian did as he was told and Firestorm again breathed out his healing blue nimbus, this time over Aurora. Elian was astonished as he felt the effects through the bond. Even though the sensations were only dimly sensed, he felt energised and full of vitality afterwards. It was incredible.

Nolita watched Ra's healing with an expression that flickered between disgust and wonder. When Firestorm had finished and moved away from Ra, she addressed Elian with barely contained anger.

'When are you going to tell me what's going on?' she grated.

'We're in a place called France,' he offered, not quite sure how much to tell her.

'France? Never heard of it. How did we get here? Even a dragon would take several days to fly out of Cemaria from where we were. I don't feel as if I've been asleep long. Wait! I remember something strange. Something was spinning – a weird hole in the air, then I was sort of swimming. No. It must have been a dream. I'm talking nonsense.' She shook her head a little as if trying to shake the strange visions loose.

'No, you're not,' Elian said quickly, noting Nolita's inadvertent use of the word 'dragon' with an inward smile. Until now, he had only ever heard her refer to dragons as 'beasts'. It was a small, but significant step. 'We came here through a sort of vortex. We're not in Areth any more. We're in another world.'

'The trees are strange,' she noted, seeming to ignore the significance of his answer. 'The sky's the wrong shade of blue. And that noise . . . what's that noise?'

Elian and Kira glanced at one another. The unspoken question between them was clear. How much should they tell Nolita? How much could she cope with?

'Don't lie to me,' she said, looking round fearfully at the dragons. 'I'm beginning to remember. You tied me up and brought me here. There's no point denying it. Come on, I'm waiting. Why are we here and what's that noise?'

She was right, Elian decided. She did deserve to know what was going on. If she was ever to trust them, they had to be honest with her.

'We brought you here because it's the shortest

way to Orupee. Aurora can open gateways into this world. When we leave tomorrow she'll open another one that'll take us straight to Orupee. We'll have saved weeks of flying time.' Elian paused a moment, because he knew she would not take the second part well.

'All right, let's assume for a moment that I believe you. Why don't we just leave now?' she asked.

'Because Ra can only open the gateways at dawn,' he replied. 'She says that's when the barrier between the worlds is weakest.' He thought about trying to explain further, but realised it was unlikely to make any difference. 'The noise you can hear is the sound of war. The people here are fighting with strange weapons that throw death over huge distances.'

Nolita looked unconvinced, but her mind was racing ahead, the noise already dismissed.

'I don't understand,' she said softly. 'You trick me, tie me up and bring me here because you want me to go to Orupee. I don't know you. I've never seen you before. It makes no sense. Why?' Nolita asked. 'My home is in Cemaria. It's that . . . the beast's idea, isn't it? It wants me to go there.'

'It's a bit more complicated than that, Nolita,' Kira said, sounding much like a mother explaining a concept to her little child. 'It's your destiny to go

189

to Orupee. You can fight it, but you can't avoid it. None of us can. If it makes you feel any better, I didn't want to be a dragonrider any more than you do. All I ever wanted was to be a hunter for my tribe.'

'A hunter?' Nolita asked.

'Yes. I remember the first time I saw the hunters coming home from the bush. They looked so fine with their faces and bodies painted for the hunt. We all raced to meet them, clapping and cheering. The celebrations made the hunters important – more important than any others in the tribe. That was enough for me.'

Kira's eyes were distant as she relived her memories.

'My elders laughed when I began to train the following day; I was barely five season rotations old. I must have looked ridiculous, prowling through the bushes with my pretend spear. I knew they were laughing at me, but I didn't care. I hounded the hunters with questions whenever I got the chance, and as I grew, so did my determination. I worked harder than anyone else, gradually getting better and better until the tribe had no choice. They had to take me seriously. I was so close when Longfang appeared. Just a few more days and I would have taken my first proper trip into the bush as a hunter

190

for my tribe. My dream died the day Fang came, but I knew I couldn't refuse him.'

'Why not? Why didn't you run and follow your own path?' Nolita asked, her voice barely more than a whisper.

'Because I couldn't deny the bond,' Kira replied, a note of anguish in her resigned statement. 'The moment Fang spoke to me in my mind, I knew we were meant to be together.'

Nolita's eyes took on a guilty look.

Kira met her eyes with a knowing gaze. 'Yes, I could have run like you did,' she continued. 'Where has it got you? You were starving, Nolita. If we hadn't found you, you would have died before another season turned. Denying destiny invites death.'

'But you're strong. You know how to hunt. You could've—'

'No,' Kira said bluntly. 'I couldn't. If I'd run then my dream would have died anyway. I wanted to be a hunter, but I couldn't have hidden Fang from my tribe. A dragon can't be denied, Nolita. If you're called, you're called. You can run, but it won't do any good. In the end the Creator will turn you back to His purpose.'

'You believe the Creator decides the bonds? That's ridiculous!' Nolita exclaimed.

'Who else can decide what's going to happen hundreds of season rotations before the day?' Kira asked.

'The King of the Underworld for one,' Nolita said quickly.

Both Elian and Kira spontaneously burst out laughing.

'What's so funny?' Nolita asked. 'I've heard lots of stories about him. Why shouldn't he be able to control the bonds?'

Elian regained his composure first.

'Sorry, Nolita,' he said. 'We shouldn't have laughed, but you just saw Firestorm heal Aurora. Before you woke up, Kira and I had also seen him heal you. The King of the Underworld doesn't have the power to heal. From what I remember he can't create and doesn't know the future. More importantly he can't read minds. He needs words to be spoken aloud. That's why Clerics drone on and on about guarding your tongue. The rider's bond with his dragon is silent until the dragon and rider meet. Your bond with Firestorm is pure.'

'But what if a beast is corrupt before he meets his rider?' Nolita persisted, her mouth set in a stubborn line.

'Weren't you listening to Elian?' Kira asked, anger in her voice. 'Think, Nolita! Dragons can only mind-speak. They don't say words aloud, so Underworld creatures have nothing to work with. The only way they can turn a dragon to evil is through you.'

Nolita's eyes widened with shock. 'Are you suggesting that I . . .'

'I'm not suggesting anything, Nolita,' Kira said, raising her hands in denial. 'I'm just giving you the facts.'

Elian watched with satisfaction as Nolita took a swift glance at the three dragons. Her eyes paused for the slightest instant on Firestorm, and Elian could see that some of the fear had gone. She still looked frightened by the proximity of the dragons, but there was a hint of self-control about her that he had not seen before.

'Here – have a drink,' he offered. 'Water should help you recover. You were unconscious for some time.'

He passed her his water bottle and she gave him a nod of gratitude. To his surprise, however, rather than lift it to her lips she poured the water over her hands. The look of intent concentration on her face as she scrubbed at her palms and nails was fierce. Nolita had taken a step forwards, but he could see she still had a long path ahead if she was ever to be comfortable as a dragonrider.

The distant rumble of war was constant throughout the afternoon, but it was not until dark fell that the true alien nature of this world became visible. From the edge of the woods an endless series of flashing lights on the eastern horizon was visible, marking the fiery explosions of weapons. Elian tried to explain to Nolita what he and Kira had seen during their last visit here, but there was no sign of comprehension in her eyes. The concepts were just beyond belief to one who had not seen them for herself.

The dragons sat guard while the three riders rested. Despite their presence, Nolita went to sleep quickly. Elian and Kira were not long in following her lead.

Chapter Sixteen
The Oracle

'It's time,' Kira announced.

The two simple words brought the terror flooding back. Nolita did not need to look at her hands. She could feel them shaking. With a groan, she slumped to the ground as all strength deserted her legs.

'I can't,' she sobbed. 'Leave me here. I can't do it.'

'Yes you can, Nolita,' Elian said firmly. 'We're not leaving you here, so you can forget that idea right now. You'd be killed for sure. Trust us. We got you here safely, didn't we? Firestorm won't leave without you. You'll be far more comfortable flying with me on Ra's back than you would in Firestorm's talons. Those are your options.'

'I'll be sick,' she sniffed, the tears still running down her cheeks and under her chin.

'If it makes you feel better, then go ahead,' he replied. 'I'd prefer you were sick now rather than later, but a little mess won't hurt me.'

'*Speak for yourself, rider. I don't take kindly to having human vomit staining my scales,*' Ra said, her tone haughty.

'*Come on, Ra! Helping Firestorm and Nolita was your idea to begin with. Don't get all high and mighty with me now.*'

Ra did not answer, but Elian could feel her disdain for Nolita's extreme behaviour.

'Would you feel safer if I tied you into the saddle like before, Nolita?' he offered. 'It's no problem.'

'I need to wash my hands.'

'You washed them five minutes ago,' Kira sighed.

'Washing helps me feel better,' Nolita insisted. 'It gives me a feeling of control. I *need* to wash my hands.'

'There's no time, Nolita. You have to come now.' Elian felt rotten for using such a commanding tone, but he knew there was no other way. He bent down and grabbed her by her right upper arm. Kira took the other arm and between them they half dragged, half carried her across to where Ra was waiting.

The closer they got to Ra, the more terrified Nolita became. She was shaking like a fish out of water, and gulping great lungfuls of air as panic gripped her. Just as they reached the dawn dragon's foreleg she retched, heaving the contents of her stomach onto the leafy mulch that covered the ground. Ra flinched slightly as her talons and foot were spattered. Her nearest eye turned to stare balefully at Elian as he and Kira continued to drag her forwards.

'I'll give you a scrub-down later,' he promised.

Ra's response felt distinctly like a *'humph'*, though he did not actually hear anything.

It was a struggle to get Nolita into the saddle. Once there, Kira made sure the terrified girl was tied on securely before climbing back down and running across to Fang. Elian climbed into position behind Nolita and put his hands around her waist. She immediately clamped her hands over his and gripped them with surprising strength.

'Don't fight me, Nolita. If you're difficult, I'll push you out of the saddle. You're tied on so you won't fall far, but Ra might find flying awkward with you dangling underneath her. Just relax, do what I tell you, and you'll be fine.'

Nolita did not answer. Instead she retched again. She did not have much left in her stomach, but what little she did have sprayed down Aurora's side.

'*Delightful!*' Ra said, her disgust washing through Elian's head in a wave. By chance Elian happened to look across at Firestorm. He would have thought it impossible for a dragon to look embarrassed until he saw Firestorm in that moment. Somehow he managed to convey the emotion in a way that was beyond anything Elian had ever seen in a human. '*Dawn is almost upon us,*' Ra continued. '*We must leave now, or wait for another day. It is vital we leave at the instant of dawn. Making such large gateways has stretched my powers to the limit. This one will have to serve as the last for a while. I will need some time to recover before I will be able to form another.*'

Elian had not realised Ra's ability to open the gateways at dawn was in question. He had felt her strain to open the gateways through the bond each time, but had not fully appreciated how draining they were to her.

'Sit tight, Nolita. Here we go,' he warned.

Ra shot forward with her customary burst of acceleration into the pre-dawn mist. As she did so, Nolita rocked back hard against Elian, who had anticipated the movement and braced forwards. Her head struck his a glancing blow that left him with a ringing in his ears and stars dancing before his eyes. Somehow, despite the unexpected clash, he hung on tightly to her and maintained their balance through the take-off run.

Fang flanked Ra on one side, with Firestorm on the other, but once airborne the three dragons shifted their relative positions until they were one behind the other. Firestorm led with Fang behind him and Ra bringing up the rear.

A strange tingling began inside Elian's body as he sensed the moment of dawn approach. At first he thought it was a symptom of his clash of heads with Nolita, but this was not restricted to his head. It thrummed through him with a resonance of power that could only have come through his link to Ra. As the sensation of vitality and strength peaked, Elian felt Ra open the gateway. As she did so, the fizz of energy he had felt the instant before was replaced by a huge sucking vortex that threatened to strip him bare. The few heartbeats before they entered the swirling gateway left Elian under no illusion as to how difficult it was for Ra to create and maintain it long enough for three dragons to pass safely through.

Elian had not experienced these sensations on previous trips through gateways. He had been vaguely aware of Ra's efforts, but this time the twisting lurch as they entered limbo was combined with the feeling that he was more a part of what was happening. His link with Ra was deepening all the time, he realised. His conclusion triggered mixed emotions. On the one hand, it felt good to be more closely allied to his life partner. On the other he realised he could now expect to feel these terrifying sensations every time they travelled through a gateway.

Emergence was accompanied by a feeling of deep mental fatigue. Elian's head hurt as if he had concentrated on something for too long, but more so. The ache was sharp and his right hand went automatically to his crown to cradle it. He felt awful, but even as the needle-like spiking inside his brain reached a peak it suddenly ceased altogether.

'*Sorry about that,*' Ra said apologetically. '*It will take me a while to recover. That was hard work.*'

'Why did it hurt so much?' Elian asked, grateful that the pain was gone. 'And what did you do to take my pain away?'

'*I've just restricted our link for a while,*' she explained. '*I've still got the pain, but there's no need for you to share in my recovery. It will be a while before I'm ready to make any more gateways. It was the first one that brought this on. If I hadn't had to form one so long from the perfect moment of dawn, I could probably have taken us back and forth several more times before needing a rest. Don't worry, I'll be fine again in a few days.*'

'A few days!' he exclaimed, not wanting to think about the pain Ra would have to bear during that time. 'Can't Firestorm heal you?'

'*Not this time, Elian. It's not that sort of hurt. But it was a good thought, thank you.*'

'But you'll be all right, won't you?'

'*Yes, Elian. I'll be fine. There's no need to worry. I just need some rest, that's all.*'

Nolita gasped. She wanted to close her eyes, but was terrified that she might fall from the dragon's back. The view was every bit as spectacular as any she had seen in Cemaria. Snow-capped mountains dominated the landscape around them. The long drop below set her heart drumming in her chest and, as she gasped great gulps of air, her head spun with vertigo. The air was crisp and clean, but also freezing cold. A stiff wind was blowing, which cut through her clothing with a cruel bite. She began shivering within a matter of heartbeats after they emerged. It's all right for Elian and Kira with their fur-lined clothing, she thought bitterly. Elian's arms were wrapped around her, but they did little to shield her from the icy blast. She was going to freeze if they did not find warmer air or shelter quickly. 'There – the ridge ahead of us,' Elian said, his voice loud in her ear.

At first she could not see what he was talking about, but as she played her eyes back and forth across the ridge two things suddenly stood out. First she saw a huge dragon. It was staring at them with bright orange eyes. She shuddered. Its body was black as coal, and lined with vicious-looking ridges and horns that gave it an evil appearance. Near to where the dark beast lurked she could see a large cave entrance high above the floor of the valley. They were heading directly towards it.

As they began their descent, they encountered one of the many dangers inherent in flying over mountainous terrain. The wind over the rocky landscape had stirred up the layers of air, making it rough with turbulence.

'Don't worry, Nolita. I've got you. Hold on tight to the pommel. Everything will be fine, I promise.' She could hear the note of fear in Elian's voice and her heart rate accelerated even further. He had always seemed so calm before. She squeezed the pommel with a death grip and tightened her thighs against the dragon's sides. For the next few minutes she was sure she was doomed to fall to her death as the dragon bucked and bounced under them like a wild stallion, intent on throwing them off his back.

Elian's arms tightened around Nolita's waist and

she clung to his promise. Her mind was blank with fear and sparkling points of light danced in her eyes as her rapid panting flooded her body with too much oxygen. The dragons and riders fought a dangerous battle through the swirling air currents all the way down to the cave mouth. Nearing the cliff-face, she caught a glimpse of a young man sitting just inside the entrance with his back against the left-hand wall.

As they approached the ledge in front of the cave, Ra suddenly dropped like a stone, falling rapidly below the level of the entrance. There was a frantic flurry of flapping as Ra dragged them back up through the vicious down-draft. The landing in front of the mouth of the cave felt clumsy and unbalanced. To Nolita's surprise, Fang and Firestorm fared little better, arriving in a most undignified manner on the ledge next to them.

The young man rose. He was tall and muscled, with a classic V-shaped torso and long blond hair tied back into a ponytail. Elian's arms had relaxed around her waist after they touched down on the ledge, but she felt them tighten slightly again as the stranger approached. One look at his cold blue eyes, square jaw and thin, curving lips and Nolita sensed Elian's reaction was one of wariness, and possibly even dislike. The response struck her as unusual. But this was the least of her worries. Her mind was fixed on one thing – getting down off the beast and as far away from it as possible.

'At last!' the young man said, walking over to Aurora's side and offering a hand to help Nolita down. 'I've been waiting to see the Oracle for three days. The Guardians told me I had to wait for more riders. What kept you?'

'That's a long story,' Elian responded, his voice flat. He slid down and landed neatly next to the stranger. 'Elian, Aurora's rider,' he said, offering his hand in a gesture of greeting.

'Pell, rider of Whispering Shadow.' The rider of the night dragon half crushed Elian's hand with a rock-like grip. 'We should go in. The Guardians are worried. There's something wrong with the Oracle.'

'So Ra tells me.' If Elian had possessed hackles they would have been up. There was a cold arrogance about Pell that made Elian want to grind his teeth. 'Pell, meet Nolita.'

Pell inclined his head towards Nolita, but addressed his question to Elian. 'So why's she riding with you? Are you together?' he asked pointedly.

'No. Nothing like that. It's complicated, so it can wait. This is Kira, rider of Longfang,' he added as Kira approached. 'We've travelled together from Racafi.'

'Good to meet you, Kira,' he replied, but his greeting held no warmth. 'Come. We must go in now. Shadow tells me it's time.'

'Of course,' she responded, glancing at Elian as Pell turned to enter the cave mouth without waiting to see if they were following. 'Lead on,' she said to his retreating back. There was an edge to Kira's voice that set danger bells ringing in Elian's head, but it felt good to know he was not alone in his initial reaction to Pell.

'Interesting chap,' Elian muttered.

Nolita appeared to be in shock from their short ride to the ledge. Elian did not blame her for the reaction. It had been frightening for him, and he had experienced several hours of flying in calm air first. He and Kira positioned themselves on either side of Nolita, lending her support as they followed Pell into the yawning chasm.

Two Guardians stepped out from either side of the cave to block Pell's path. One wore mail of silver with a blue tabard sporting a white dragon motif. The other wore armour of black with a gold tabard bearing a black dragon.

'Halt!' the Guardians ordered in unison, crossing their spears in a gesture that was clear. 'Why do you approach the Oracle?'

Pell stopped and placed his hands upon his hips.

'It's my time,' he responded. 'Time and past time. The others are here now. Can we enter?'

As Elian, Kira and Nolita approached, the Guardians looked across at each other as if seeking reassurance. A slight noise behind Elian caused him to look around. The dragons were following in single file, with the fearsome-looking night dragon leading. He hoped Nolita did not look back.

'The Oracle awaits you,' the Guardians said together. They turned aside, returning to their positions on either side of the passageway. As Elian watched them resume their posts, he realised they were dragonriders. Their dragons were there too, watching from great recesses carved into the cave walls.

'*How were the Guardians chosen, Ra?*' he asked silently.

'*Do I sense you are concerned that we may find ourselves in such a role?*' she answered. '*Do not fear, Elian. We are not suited to such a life-purpose. There is adventure ahead of us. I feel it.*'

'*But they were chosen by the Oracle, weren't they?*'

'*Yes.*'

The answer was not reassuring. The fact that the Oracle could issue a dragon with such a binding life-purpose on both rider and dragon made him wonder exactly what sort of role was pre-destined for him and Ra.

The light in the cave gradually reduced as they moved deeper into the mountainside. Occasional torches burned in brackets fixed to the walls. They had not walked far when the cave widened abruptly, opening into a vast underground chamber. A rocky path descended ahead of them on a zigzagging ramp to the chamber floor. More torches burned on the walls and on cast-iron posts, but despite the flickering light of dozens of torches the roof and far reaches of the chamber were lost in dark shadows. Strange random pillars of rock twisted from the floor of the chamber, climbing up into the darkness high above. Great stalactites and stalagmites gave the impression of teeth in the mouths of side chambers, whilst the occasional gleam of reflected light hinted at possible wealth hidden within the cave's walls.

Fascinating shapes and teasing shadows would have demanded attention at any other time, but the eyes of both dragons and riders were drawn as one to a circular hole in the cavern floor. Someone had constructed a low decorative wall around it, with a variety of intricate dragon statuettes standing at regular intervals on the top. It had a diameter that would take a man five long paces to cross and from its depths twisted a strange, luminous, curling vapour.

The smoke pulsed and swirled with light, but showed no signs of dispersing into the vastness of the chamber. Instead it hung, slowly curling in twisting eddies, fashioning and dissolving hints of familiar shapes in nebulous form.

The four riders, followed by their dragons, descended the great ramp until they approached the shimmering column of smoky light.

'*Is this . . .*' Elian began.

'*The Oracle – yes,*' Ra answered, her mental voice full of awe.

As they stopped in front of the Oracle there was a noise, a whisper of sound much like the faint slithering hiss of a snake crossing stony ground. Elian's breath caught in his throat. Could this Oracle speak aloud, or would it speak within his mind as Aurora did?

'I am dying.'

It was a whisper, but a whisper that held the power to penetrate. The young people gazed into the writhing smoke and were startled as the misty substance shifted into the shape of a face. It was the face of a great dragon with eyes of fire.

'I am dying,' it repeated. 'To ye four partnerships falls the burden of my restoration. I charge thee with thy life purpose, dragons and riders both. Thine is the Great Quest. Twice before have I issued this charge: twice the restoration has failed. This is the final chance. If thrice this charge should fail, then I shall pass to the Otherworld and the purpose of dragonkind will die. I cannot see your destiny in this. Such knowledge is denied. What help and foresight I can give is contained in this verse. Consider it well.'

The Oracle's voice faded and the shape of the dragon's head began to disperse. *'What verse?'* they all wondered. *'What did the Oracle mean?'* Suddenly a booming thought inside everyone's heads answered the question.

'Beyond time's bright arrow, life-saving breath,
Love's life-force giving, slays final death.
Orbs must be given, four all in all.
Orbs to renew me, stilling death's call.

'Delve 'neath the surface, life's transport hides,
Healing, restoring – bright river tides.
Enter the sun's steps; shed no more tears.
Attain ye the orb; vanquish the fears.

'Release the dark orb – death brings me life.
Take brave ones' counsel, 'ware ye the knife.

Exercise caution, stay pure and heed,
Yield unto justice: truth will succeed.

   'Ever protected, the dusk orb lies
   Behind the cover, yet no disguise.
   Afterlife image, unreal yet real,
   Lives in the shadows, waits to reveal.

'Life after death from death before life,
Enter the new age, through deadly strife.
Greatest of orbs is — dragon's device.
Gifted for ever: life's sacrifice.'

The voice stopped. Elian blinked several times, his thoughts awash with confusion. He sensed that Ra was similarly baffled by the strange verses.

'*What was* that *all about?*' he asked her, hoping she would understand the meaning of the twisted rhymes.

Ra did not answer. Suddenly the shape of the great dragon's head re-formed in the smoke, its fiery eyes seeming to look directly into Elian's. For a moment it seemed that the Oracle saw through to the very core of his being. The close scrutiny made him feel naked, small and insignificant; his soul laid bare for the Oracle's inspection. To his relief the sensation did not last long, for its gaze shifted across

210

the group, pausing briefly to regard each in turn.

'The answers ye seek are in the words I have given ye,' the giant whispering voice said. 'Heed them well, for they will lead ye along the path of that purpose for which ye were created. I can lend ye no special strength with which to face the trials ahead. Ye have what ye need. But beware! Only in unity will ye find the strength to prevail. Enmities must be put aside. Day, night, dawn and dusk must work together in this if ye art to succeed. I charge ye now to swear on whatsoever oath ye do hold most dear. Pledge to be true and to hold together as one. Do ye swear?'

'I do so swear.' The words were out of Elian's mouth before he realised he had uttered them. The presence of the Oracle was so powerful that he doubted he had the will to deny its order, even had he tried with all his heart. Around him and in his mind he heard his fellow riders and Aurora echoing the oath.

'It is well. Do not delay. My presence fades. The orbs must be brought with all speed. Each orb ye bring will purchase more time, but if I do not receive the final orb by the harvest full moon I shall fail and pass on. On ye depends the future of dragonkind. The purpose that has held dragons to the noble path for millennia lives or dies with me.'

Chapter Seventeen
Dragon Pact

'Come,' Pell commanded as the four riders neared the mouth of the Oracle's cave. 'Follow me.'

'What gives you the right to give orders?' Kira challenged, her eyes flashing with irritation. One look at Kira's expression and Elian was glad he was not standing in Pell's boots. The Racafian girl was tough as nails. It would take a fool to face her down when she was in this mood.

'I am clearly the eldest,' he replied, oblivious to the danger signals. 'I've seen sixteen rotations. It's obvious I should lead. Besides, I've found a good campsite nearby.'

'Offal!' Kira retorted, her voice sharp. 'If the oldest is going to lead, we should listen to Fang. He's the oldest dragon here. All of the dragons are older and more experienced than we are. Why should it be a rider who leads? The Oracle seemed more dragon than human.'

It was a good point, Elian realised. He had automatically started thinking about the challenge they had been set. The verses were baffling. He knew he was unlikely to unravel any meaning from them. If anyone could solve such riddling words, it would be a dragon. Dragons were renowned for their clarity of thought, and for wisdom born from long years of worldly experience. This was a dragon problem. It was logical that a dragon should lead. To his surprise, Nolita interrupted the brewing conflict.

'We made a promise – a pact – to work together,' she said tentatively. '"*Only in unity will ye find the strength to prevail.*" We don't need a leader. We need to agree.'

'Nolita's right,' Elian said quickly, recognising the good sense in her words. 'Kira, Pell's already found a campsite. Let's go and take a look. Staying here's just wasting precious time. We'll need to work together to solve the riddles and get the orbs before the harvest moon.'

'Fine then,' Kira conceded reluctantly. 'We'll follow Pell to this campsite of his. The flight will give us all some time to think.'

Kira gave Pell a final withering look before

leaping up Fang's side and into her saddle. She was so annoyed with the night dragon's rider that she gave no thought to getting Nolita back into a dragon saddle. Nolita felt emboldened by the encounter with the Oracle. Something inside her had changed. She could feel it. When the great dragon face had appeared in the misty smoke she knew she should have been a quivering wreck on the floor. Instead all fear had slipped from her like a cast-off robe and she had felt strong – strong and bold. The giant whispering voice had spoken to them all, but in her head it had also spoken words of encouragement with an authority unlike any she had ever encountered before.

It was strange. Nolita could not remember what the Oracle had said to her in secret, but the echoes of its whispering voice had a lingering effect. Could she really be what the Oracle wanted? Could she ride a dragon and complete a quest of great importance? Would she become a heroine like the ones she had always loved to hear about in stories?

She looked at Firestorm. He was hers and she was his. She knew she could not deny it any more. But although they had not yet left the Oracle's cave, the bravery she had felt in the presence of the powerful spirit creature was already fading. She took a step towards her dragon. He was watching her intently and she could feel his excitement through the bond. He wanted her to ride him. She took another step, but then the flood of revulsion and fear swept over her again with renewed ferocity.

Nausea gripped her and she turned with her head in her hands.

'No. I can't do it. I'm not strong enough.' Nolita's voice was barely more than a whisper, but Elian heard every word.

'Yes you can, Nolita,' he said, misunderstanding. 'Listen, I know the ride here was frightening. To be honest it scared the hell out of me as well. But not all flying is like that. It's normally smooth and predictable. It's hard to describe how wonderful it can be. Come on – don't miss out. Besides, I can't leave you here. There's nowhere for you to go. Climbing down would be impossible. Did you see the cliffs as we landed?'

'I tried not to look,' she admitted.

'Well trust me, the drop from the ledge outside the cave was vertical for several hundred spans. Let's get on Ra's back here. That way you won't see how high up we are until we're airborne. As I see it, Ra's your only way down unless you ask Firestorm to take you.'

Does Elian know how close I came to that? she

wondered. She sighed and turned to eye Aurora with a mixture of suspicion and fear.

Elian could almost see the wheels turning in her mind. He watched her expression as she cast a glance back at Firestorm. There was a look of sadness about him. Was it guilt that made her look away so quickly, or continuing fear?

'*I will not give up on you, Nolita,*' Firestorm whispered in her mind. '*You are strong enough. The Oracle knows you are. I know you are. I'll be ready when you are.*'

Elian took her hand gently in his. She was shaking. 'Come on,' he said, keeping his voice soft. 'I'll tie you to the saddle again. It'll help you feel safer.'

Tears rolled down Nolita's cheeks, but she nodded and allowed him to help her climb up Ra's foreleg and into the saddle. She minimised touching Ra's scales with her hands. The feel of them brought a sour taste to the back of her throat and the dizziness she had felt when flying in towards the cave threatened to start again the moment she settled into the saddle.

Elian was amazed by her reaction. He loved touching his dragon's scales. He felt it incredible that someone could find the sensation repulsive.

Elian hoped fervently that Nolita would not be

sick this time, but with the wind playing across the mouth of the cave, the launch from the ledge was unlikely to be into smooth air. Taking care not to tie the rope too tightly around Nolita's body, he secured her to the saddle and climbed up behind her.

'Hold on tight, Nolita,' he said gently. 'This will probably be a bit rough again. Be brave. It won't last long.'

Elian gave Ra the mental nod that they were ready to launch. Kira and Pell were already airborne on their dragons. In the tunnel behind them Firestorm waited patiently. The day dragon would follow once they were in the air. Elian knew this was not going to be a typical launch as there was no room for Ra to extend her wings whilst they were in the cave. The only time she would be able to stretch them out wide would be when they reached the ledge, by which time they would have run out of acceleration room.

'*I'll try not to drop too far from the ledge when we launch,*' Ra assured him, backing up a few more steps.

'Good,' Elian replied, '*because if you do, I'll not be surprised to see Nolita throw up whatever's left in her stomach. She's petrified, Ra, and I've got to admit that I don't blame her. I'm feeling a little scared myself. It's* one thing to fall off a cliff, but we're about to deliberately run and jump off one. You've got wings, but I haven't, so I can't help feeling this is an insane thing to do.'

Ra gave a snort of amusement and then shot forward with the fastest acceleration Elian had yet experienced. As they emerged into full daylight Elian took a sharp intake of breath, and felt Nolita do the same as Ra leaped from the ledge. The dragon's wings snapped out to full stretch in the blink of an eye. There was the slightest of lurches as she dropped until the lift from her wings increased enough for her to settle into a stable glide. The drop lasted but a split heartbeat, yet it was sufficient to trigger a piercing scream from Nolita.

'Relax, Nolita,' Elian shouted in her ear. 'Your screaming might break Ra's concentration. I don't want her to crash because of a silly distraction.'

Ra had used the trick effectively on him during his first flight, and it worked just as well on Nolita. She clamped her jaw shut tight and gripped the front saddle horn with all her might. The air in the high mountain valley was still turbulent. They bounced and lurched through the tricky up and down drafts, following the two dragons ahead.

Ra gradually caught up with Fang and Shadow, and Firestorm moved forwards to settle into a formation position alongside them. The turbulence calmed abruptly as the four dragons flew out of the tight valley throat and into a wider, less extreme valley beyond. Pell and Shadow turned to the left and descended towards an extensive area of woodland in the broad valley basin. The other dragons followed. Within a minute or two they all landed gently in the meadow next to the eastern edge of the woods where a stream emerged from the trees.

No sooner had Ra landed than Elian began to help Nolita out of the saddle. He knew she would be keen to get off Ra's back as swiftly as possible, and he could feel that Ra was eager for the same result.

On reaching the ground Nolita staggered across to the stream, fell to her knees and began scrubbing her hands with fearsome vigour in the clear water. The frenzied cleaning clearly brought her comfort.

Kira went to the edge of the woodland to take a look around. Pell followed a few paces behind her, his strutting gait oozing self-confidence. Elian strode to intercept them, anticipating an explosion if he was not at hand to mediate.

'It's a good spot,' Kira conceded grudgingly to Elian as he approached. She gave Pell a sideways glance and Pell's lips twitched for a moment into an expression that Elian interpreted as smug satisfaction. 'The water looks clean,' Kira observed. 'The tree canopy is dense and there's plenty of material to build a shelter. I've already seen rabbit and deer, and there's lots of bird life. We can send the dragons out hunting whilst we build our shelter and set a fire. What do you say, Elian?'

'I'm fine with that, but what do the dragons say?' Elian asked, deliberately furthering Kira's earlier point about dragons being equal to humans.

'We should stop here. Thinking time would be useful. Firestorm agrees,' Ra said.

'Ra and Firestorm are in favour,' Elian relayed aloud.

'Fang too.'

'And Shadow,' Pell said. 'A shelter won't take long to build if we all help. Is Nolita all right? She seems a little strange. Is all that washing necessary?'

'It is to her,' Kira snapped. 'Washing helps her cope. Her fears are so strong they stop her enjoying things that we take for granted. Unfortunately her worst fears are of dragons and heights. She's done well to get this far.'

Pell burst out laughing. To Elian and Kira his laughter sounded cruel.

'This isn't funny,' Elian said, with cold frankness, forcing himself to contain his irritation within a mental wall of ice. 'Nolita had to face something that terrified her to get here today. Are you as brave?'

'I fear nothing,' Pell said, glaring at Elian with anger in his eyes as if the mere suggestion that he might suffer fear was a deadly insult.

'Only a fool fears nothing,' Kira retorted quickly. 'Even the bravest hunter is scared sometimes. It's his ability to turn fears into strengths that makes him brave.'

Elian ground his teeth with frustration. Kira seemed set on antagonising Pell with every sentence. It did not take the wisdom of a dragon to see that the label of 'fool' would not sit well with him. Without care, their fragile pact would be destroyed before they had begun. To his surprise, however, Pell did not rise to the bait this time. Instead he fixed Kira with his icy eyes and stared. If Kira was intimidated she did not show it.

'Listen!' Elian said firmly. 'We all have our differences. Live with it. All this arguing isn't getting us anywhere.' With a flash of surprised insight he recognised some of his father's inflections in his speech. 'Kira, I know you're skilled at woodcraft. If Pell and I collect the makings of a shelter, can you begin clearing a suitable site and start building with what we bring you? Nolita can start collecting firewood and I'll ask Ra to coordinate a hunt. I'm sure the dragons will be able to bring us plenty of fresh meat.'

With clear tasks to perform, the group worked quickly and efficiently. Pell and Elian began by finding and stripping straight branches to build a framework for the shelter. Kira scouted the area until she found a suitably flat space between two trees and not too far from the stream. Pell brought a long, straight branch that proved perfect to form the main supporting bar. This she lashed horizontally between the two trees at waist height. Then she sorted the rest of the branches and trimmed them to appropriate lengths with her belt knife.

Over the next hour she constructed a lattice framework between the crossbar and the ground that formed a one-sided roof, leaving a wedge-shaped shelter underneath. With the framework complete, the four young people set to collecting ferns and large leaves. These they placed in overlapping layers, all pointing tip downwards, over the framework. Layer upon layer went on until not the slightest glimmer of light could be seen through it from beneath. Then they collected more ferns and bracken and piled the fronds in a thick carpet inside the shelter to act as an insulating layer between their bodies and the ground.

The shelter took almost half a day to complete.

Once finished, Pell and Elian stacked the firewood that Nolita had collected and supplemented it with larger branches, too large for her to manage alone. Kira also found several sources of dry tinder. When she was satisfied that they had plenty of wood on hand to sustain the fire through the evening, she lit the fire and set a pot of water to boil.

By this time it was late afternoon and they relaxed for a while in silence. They watched the dancing flames and listened to the crackling of the wood, all thinking through the words of the Oracle and trying to decipher them.

A whoosh of air overhead heralded the return of the dragons. To Pell's obvious pleasure, it was Shadow who deposited a sheep at the edge of the trees. Pell and Elian worked together to butcher the carcass, removing the best cuts. If they had cured it, there would have been enough meat to last more than a week, but they took only enough for the next couple of days. Shadow obligingly finished off the remains, bones and all.

Later, sitting around the fire with full stomachs as dusk faded into night, they discussed the meaning of the Oracle's riddles.

'Well I'd say the first verse sets the scene and gives us a sort of summary of our task,' Kira offered. 'Listen:

'Beyond time's bright arrow, life-saving breath,
'Love's life-force giving, slays final death.

'I might be wrong, but it just seems to say that we're supposed to "slay the final death" of the Oracle. What do you think? It would be good to hear the dragons' thoughts on it too.'

Nolita shivered at the suggestion and sat with her arms crossed, rocking gently and hugging herself. Heartbeats passed silently, but no one had anything to add.

'Ra suggests that "Love's life-force giving," could be to do with us accepting the Oracle's task. You know, that it's our life purpose,' Elian offered eventually.

'That makes sense,' Pell replied. 'Of course the next two lines are easy,' he continued quickly.

'Orbs must be given, four all in all.
'Orbs to renew me, stilling death's call.

'Our task is to find the four Orbs and give them to the Oracle. This will somehow stop it from dying.'

'Genius,' Kira muttered, rolling her eyes.

'Kira! Don't start again. Remember the Oracle said if we don't work together we'll fail,' Elian warned. 'So there are four orbs – does anyone have any clues as to what the orbs are like? What are we looking for?'

'Well there are four following verses and each seems to talk about a different orb,' Kira offered. 'Each orb looks like it's linked to one of the four breeds of dragon in the order day, night, dusk and dawn.'

This time it was Pell who rolled his eyes in an exaggerated imitation of Kira.

Elian ignored him. 'Agreed,' he said. 'Let's try to make sense of the first. *Delve 'neath the surface, life's transport hides.* Does anyone understand that? It doesn't mean much to me.'

'*Delve 'neath the surface* sounds like it might be talking about caves, or mines,' Pell suggested. '*Delving* makes me think of digging deep underground. And *life's transport* could be a dragon, or dragons. We are dragonriders, after all. Our transport for the rest of our lives will be dragons. I was taught that dragons hatch in caves and live underground for some time before setting off into the world on their journeys.'

Kira pursed her lips and her eyebrows drew together in a frown as she considered his interpretation. 'So you think there might be a dragon somewhere in a deep cave who's guarding the first orb?' she asked.

'I don't know. I'm just trying to guess at some possible meanings. Do you have a better idea?' he asked, leaning back on one arm whilst casually spearing another piece of meat with his knife. His eyes held an unspoken challenge as he waited for her response.

'No, I don't, but something about it being a dragon in a cave doesn't ring true,' she said eventually.

'Of course not,' Pell scoffed. 'It was *my* suggestion. Admit it, Kira, you don't *want* me to be right.'

'Offal!' she snapped. 'Even if that was true, I'm not fool enough to push aside the right answer just because I don't like it.'

Elian sighed loudly. 'For goodness' sake, will you two cut it out! Nolita, do you have any ideas?'

The blond girl shook her head quickly. She remained staring into the flames and rocking back and forth, her knuckles white where they gripped her sides.

'All right, if no one's got any more ideas on those lines,' Pell said, seizing the initiative, 'let's go on: *Healing, restoring – bright river tides.* Any ideas on this? I reckon the first two words probably describe the effect of the orb on the Oracle, but *bright river tides?* What's that all about?'

No one had anything to offer.

'What about the next line then?' Pell started, but

whatever he was going to say next went unsaid as a wail of anguish broke from Nolita's lips.

'Nooooooo!'

'What's the matter, Nolita? What's the matter?' Elian asked urgently.

Kira leaned to place a comforting hand on the girl's shoulder, but Nolita shrugged it away. 'Don't touch me!' she snarled. 'Stay away from me. This can't be happening. It can't be true.'

'What can't be true, Nolita?' Elian persisted gently. 'What's wrong?'

'It's Fire— the voice of the beast in my head,' she sobbed, almost naming her dragon for the first time in her distress. 'It says it knows what the next two lines mean. It says they relate to me. It's a lie! It has to be!' With that she staggered to her feet, stumbled away from the fire and ran off into the darkness weeping bitterly.

'Let her go,' Elian said, restraining Pell as he moved to follow her. 'She won't run far, and Firestorm can always find her for us when we need to leave. Ra, could you ask Firestorm what he told her, please?'

'*Of course, Elian.*' There was a pause. '*Ah, it's no wonder that Nolita is upset,*' she said a moment later. 'Enter the sun's steps; shed no more tears. Attain ye the orb; vanquish the fears. *Firestorm tells me there's a special chamber at the enclave of the day dragons called the Sun's Steps. He feels the lines are a personal message to Nolita. If so, then the task of attaining the day orb is to be hers, but in order to attain the orb she'll have to stop crying and overcome her fears.'*

Elian related Firestorm's words to the others.

'This Sun's Steps cavern wouldn't happen to be the home of a dragon by any chance?' Pell asked, glancing across at Kira with a distinctly smug expression.

'I don't know,' Elian replied, 'but there's only one sure way to find out.'

Chapter Eighteen
Breaking Point

'I'm not coming,' Pell stated.

Elian and Kira looked first at Pell, and then at one another. For a moment Elian thought he must have misheard what Pell had said, but as his memory played back the words he realised he had heard correctly.

'Why on Areth not?' he asked. 'We're supposed to work together, aren't we?'

'Work together, yes, but that doesn't mean we have to travel together. Me and Shadow wouldn't be welcome at the day dragon enclave. There's always been trouble between day and night dragons. If we came, who knows what might happen? We're not going to risk it. We'd be foolish to try. And despite what you might think, Kira, I'm no fool.'

'Frightened, are we?' Kira asked, her voice

carrying a taunting edge that made Elian throw his hands in the air with frustration.

'I told you, Kira, I'm not afraid of anything,' Pell retorted angrily. 'It's not about fear. It's about common sense. Go to the chamber. Get the orb with Nolita. I'll start looking for the night orb. Nolita's going to need your help to complete her part of the quest. I'm going find the *brave ones* at the enclave of the night dragons and see what they can tell me about the night orb.'

'Are you sure that's what the lines in the third verse mean?' Elian asked, his voice laced with doubt. 'No offence, but I would have thought the *brave ones* were the day dragons.'

'Ha! And I suppose you'll hold up Nolita as proof of this?' Pell scoffed.

A deafening roar from one of the nearby dragons made all three riders jump.

'*What's going on? What's wrong?*' Elian asked Ra in a flash.

'*Firestorm is letting Pell know that he disapproves of anyone slurring his rider. He stands ready to defend her.*'

'*Well tell him to back down. Pell doesn't understand Nolita. He's tactless, but I don't think he's out to start a fight,*' Elian projected. 'It's not good to speak badly of a dragonrider when her dragon's around, Pell,' he continued aloud. 'Firestorm might not be as big

230

as Shadow, but I wouldn't like to see what he could do if he became really angry.'

A flash of doubt passed across Pell's face, but he was quick to regain his composure after a rapid mental exchange with his dragon.

'Shadow's not afraid of Firestorm,' he said. 'Nor am I. We'll leave in the morning. I expect to return to the Oracle with the night orb within the fortnight.'

'What about the first line of that verse, Pell?' Kira asked. 'The lines seem full of hidden meanings, but I don't like the sound of *death brings me life*. Whatever the rest of the third verse means, I've got a bad feeling about that phrase. I think it would be safer to look for one orb at a time. A quest like this sounds great – full of excitement and adventure. The thing is, in lots of the quest stories I've heard, people die. It doesn't matter what we think of one another. We've all got different strengths and weaknesses. If we work together, we'll stand a better chance of getting through this thing alive.'

'I agree,' Elian said. 'I don't like the idea of splitting up. How would we know if you failed? We could end up wasting time trying to find you.'

'That's offal, and you know it!' Pell responded, his stance defensive and set. 'Whoever gets back to the Oracle first can leave a message for the others.

231

If the Oracle won't relay it, then the Guardians will. I'm not going to the enclave of the day dragons and that's final. I suggest you worry about how to help Nolita get brave enough to beat her fears. From what I've seen, it won't be easy.'

Nolita ran from the campfire and into the forest, but she had not gone more than fifty paces before new fears assaulted her. It was dark under the trees – very dark. There were strange noises and smells that ignited her imagination with thoughts of stalking predators and unknown dangers lurking behind every tree. She stopped. Her heart hammered. When she turned she could see the glow of the campfire, warm and friendly. To go much further would mean being blind and alone. It would be easy to get lost.

She sank down against the trunk of a tree and began to cry. Tears streamed down her face as deep sobs of misery shook her to the core. She so wanted to be brave like her brother Balard, who would have made a fine dragonrider, or her sister, Sable, who seemed as fearless as Nolita was fearful. Why was she cursed with being different? It was so unfair.

The Oracle had conveyed its trust in her during the moment it had held her in its gaze. She had felt its faith course through her and for that short time she had felt as if she could face anything. Now, however, that feeling had long gone and she felt small, alone and vulnerable again. The weight of the Oracle's charge hung heavy on her heart. She felt neither worthy of its trust, nor capable of seeing the quest through.

Three times now she had ridden on a dragon's back. Despite her fears, and the turbulent conditions, no harm had come to her. Why was she still terrified?

Just thinking about flying brought to mind the sensation of touching the dragon's scales. Suddenly she felt unclean again. The instinct to wash her hands was overwhelming. The stream was the other side of the campsite, but if she moved carefully, she could reach it without alerting the others to her presence.

The beast would know, of course. She could feel its presence in her head. It seemed to be there constantly, lurking in the dark recesses of her mind. Would it tell the others? If they came after her she would run. She desperately needed to be alone. It had been bad enough when she had been on the run from the beast. Now she had to cope with the added pressure of this strange quest.

The others seemed so perfectly suited to this sort of thing. Elian, with his obvious hunger for adventure and his love of flying, was in his element. Kira was tough and at home in the wild. She was so fierce at times that Nolita was sure lions would run if they saw her coming. Then there was Pell: tall and strong, calm and self-confident. Why then was it her destiny to face the Oracle's first challenge? If this was the Creator's will, He had a sick sense of humour.

'Mother and Father would have a fit if they knew you were thinking such blasphemy, Nolita,' she chided herself. 'Come on. Pull yourself together.'

Dashing the tears from her cheeks, she climbed back to her feet and leaned against the tree to gather her composure. Steadier in mind and body, she skirted around the campsite and headed down towards the stream.

It took a little while, but she moved so silently that the others were not aware of her. The beasts were all some distance away and were unlikely to bother her until the riders were ready to leave in the morning.

Plunging her hands into the cold, clear water was bliss and she could feel her body relaxing as soon as she began the familiar ritual. Nolita set to scrubbing her hands vigorously, taking care to avoid making any noise. As she washed, her thoughts drifted back to the moment when the Oracle held her in its gaze and she had felt brave enough to face any danger. Was it possible? Could the Oracle have furnished her with a hidden measure of bravery? If so, how could she access it?

Dipping her hands back into the cold mountain stream, she suddenly noticed the silvery reflection of the great moon shimmering on the surface of the water. It had been there all along, but she had been too preoccupied to notice. The sky was totally clear of cloud. The two minor moons and the stars burned with breathtaking brilliance. Awestruck, she reclined on the bank and gazed up into the infinite depths of space, lost in wonder at the vast number of stars lighting the heavens.

Ever since she was a little girl, she had enjoyed a special relationship with the stars. It had started when one of the elders from her village had sat with her one evening and told her a story of how the Creator had made the heavens and the world. The kindly old man sat by her side and asked her what she could see in the sky. When she described the patterns she saw, he told her that there had not always been so many stars. 'Each star is actually a departed soul set in the sky by the Creator's hand,' he said. 'He puts them there to shower the world with the light of all the good things in the departed person's heart. Some burn brighter than others, but they're all there if you look hard enough.'

The old man had passed away not long afterwards. 'Can I see his star?' she wondered. 'Such a lovely old man would surely have a really bright one.'

She smiled at the thought. It was nonsense, of course, but the man's words had brought her comfort. She liked the idea that when her life in this world was over, something of her might live on indefinitely. If she believed with all her heart that the death of her body would not be the end, then many of her fears would become irrelevant and fade away. Would she ever feel such certainty? Others managed it, but then, others were brave.

Nolita had trodden the circular arguments before, but this time they felt different. The encounter with the Oracle had changed her somehow and these logical conclusions did not seem so pointless any more. A feeling of progress gave her a glimmer of hope that warmed her inside.

'The least I can do is to try to complete my part of the quest,' she whispered. 'I'm not alone, and my brave companions can help me.'

She began to get up with the intention of returning quietly to the campsite, but a stealthy movement on the other side of the stream caused her to freeze.

Cold clamped her gut and her breath seized in her chest as she realised something was creeping towards her through the darkness. All thoughts of bravery vanished. A wave of goosepimples raised the hairs on her arms and her mouth felt suddenly dry. What was it? What predators stalked Orupee?

She concentrated hard on remaining totally still and watching for further hints of movement. As she watched, she saw not one, but several dark shadows moving forwards in a line. It was well that her eyes were adjusted to the dark, as it helped her to identify the shapes. They were human. What was more, they were all carrying spears.

Chapter Nineteen
Attack

It took a heartbeat or two for Nolita to realise what the men were doing. Their movements were cautious and silent. They were hunting the beasts.

For a moment her heart surged with excitement. If they killed the beast, then she would be free of him for ever. As soon as the thought entered her mind she realised she had to stop them. If the hunters killed the beasts, then the Oracle would die. Despite her fears she really wanted to help the Dragon Spirit. Through the Oracle hope had been reborn in her heart. She was not ready to risk losing that hope before it had time to grow.

What would Elian or Kira do now? she thought. Would they shout a warning, or run to fetch help? No. That would just alert the hunters that they'd been discovered. The answer was simple, but she instinctively shied away from it. She would have to speak with the beast through the mind contact they shared. The problem was that she did not know how.

'Concentrate, Nolita,' she breathed, willing her heart and mind to be still. 'Just concentrate on the beast and think your warning to him.'

'*Beast?*' she thought, focusing her mind as totally as she could on the name. 'F . . . *Firestorm, can you hear me?*'

'*Yes, Nolita,*' Firestorm responded immediately, clearly surprised by her call. '*Your mental voice is strong. I can hear you clearly.*'

'*You're in danger. There are hunters near the stream. They're coming closer,*' she projected, strangely pleased to have anything she did described as 'strong'.

'*Dragonhunters! Try to remain hidden. I'll alert the others and we'll get you to safety as soon as we can. Can you tell how many there are?*'

'*No,*' she replied. '*I can see a line of them. I'd guess at least a dozen.*'

'*A large party! Your warning may have saved us all. Thank you, Nolita.*'

Tears welled in Nolita's eyes. Firestorm's voice had sounded proud. It had been a long time since anyone had been proud of anything she had done.

She should feel unclean after speaking to the dragon, but for once the instinct to wash did not touch her, and the sense of freedom this brought felt wonderful.

Husam crept forwards, spear at the ready. The hulking shadow of Tembo to his right calmed some of his jitters. The big man's presence had always given him comfort. Husam had looked forward to this attack with excited anticipation, but now the moment was approaching, he could not shake off the bad feelings that haunted his conscience.

To reach this valley had taken three weeks of the most gruelling travel that Husam had ever known. Kasau had pushed the party relentlessly, to the point where Husam suspected the strange man had become obsessed beyond reason. Several of the party had given up and turned aside, unable to cope with the punishing pace. Kasau had let them go without a word. The remaining hunters had ridden halfway across one continent, sailed over a sea and penetrated deep into a second. Aside from the sea voyage, which had lasted two days, Husam had enjoyed no more than a couple of hours' rest each day. He felt tired, but the adrenaline flowing through his body as the hunt neared its conclusion heightened his senses, giving him a feeling of alertness that he hoped was not false.

How Kasau had tracked the dawn dragon here was still a mystery. However, the strange hunter appeared to have a sixth sense when it came to dragons. If he said the dawn dragon was here, then Husam would not question him. Kasau had proved his abilities on more than one occasion.

A sudden noise caused Husam to look up. A dragon was getting airborne. The unmistakable sound of huge wingbeats caused his heart to leap. Had the dragons detected their presence? Had they travelled all this way only to have their prey escape at the last moment? No. He could only hear a single set of wingbeats. Squinting, he could just make out the dark outline of another dragon ahead.

He paused, looking down the line to his left to see if Kasau would relay instructions. A few heartbeats later the man to his left gave a series of exaggerated hand signals. The light from the moons and stars was plenty for him to be able to see and interpret the signals. 'Target ahead. Continue.'

So the dawn dragon is still on the ground, he thought. Even if we lose the dusk dragon through bad timing, the dawn dragon is the kill of choice.

A stream cut across the meadow in front of him. The water was not wide or deep, but it had eroded a steep-sided course across the field, the banks of which were about as deep as the average man was tall. Taking care not to make any noise, he slipped silently down the bank to the water's edge. It was easy enough to cross silently, though he did hear a slight splash to his right. It was Tembo. He had jumped the stream comfortably, but where he had landed was slick with moisture and one of his feet had slipped back into the water. Given Kasau's obsession with this hunt it was probably a good thing that Tembo was out towards the end of the line. He winced. Had the big man been closer to Kasau, their leader might have killed him for his error.

As he eased up the far bank of the stream, Husam could clearly see the outline of their target ahead. A quick glance to right and left revealed that the line was reforming at the top of the bank. This was it.

It took a moment or two for the stragglers to get to the top of the bank. Kneeling, he waited for the final signal. The man to his left raised a hand. He raised his left in an imitation of the signal and glanced right to make sure Tembo was similarly poised. To his left the man's hand dropped and he began to move forwards swiftly and silently as the final charge began. Husam dropped his hand and was up and running a split heartbeat later, but as he leaped forward his doubts suddenly swelled within him like an abscess, the pressure building rapidly until it threatened to burst.

A huge roar split the air as the dragon sensed their approach and the dawn dragon's outline suddenly began to glow with rapidly increasing brilliance. Back in Racafi, the hunters who had been unfortunate enough to look at the dawn dragon when she had done this before had seen spots before their eyes for days afterwards. Some still complained of blind areas in their vision now. Husam had no intention of letting the dragon damage his eyesight, so he lowered his eyes to focus on the ground directly in front of him. He found the light from the dawn dragon was actually helpful, as he could see every lump and bump in the ground ahead.

'*Throw!*' the call from Kasau was loud and filled with triumph. Husam drew his arm back, and squinting into the now brilliant light, he hurled his spear with all his might towards the body of the dragon. A rapid series of grunts from either side of him told him that the rest of the hunters had likewise loosed their weapons.

There was a breathless pause for no more than a heartbeat before chaos erupted. The light from the dawn dragon suddenly dimmed to a bearable level. Simultaneously a monstrous jet of flame erupted, seemingly from the body of the dawn dragon, to consume the flight of hurled spears. All the weapons had wooden shafts tipped with dragonhorn except that of Kasau, which was made totally from dragonhorn, tip and shaft. There was little short of molten lava that could melt dragonbone, but the shafts of the majority of the weapons disintegrated in an instant within that flaming inferno, leaving the tips to fall harmlessly short. The only weapon that sailed on in a deadly arc was Kasau's.

Husam, shielding his eyes against the flare of fire, followed its flight. He held his breath as it dived towards its target, but just as he thought it must strike home, the dawn dragon's tail whipped around and swatted it aside with immaculate timing. For a moment he was stunned. He froze, unable to move as his mind tried to grapple with what had just happened.

The dawn dragon roared again; a deafening bellow of defiance as she turned to face the hunters. To Husam's amazement, from behind her arose the shape of a second dragon that strutted around to stand alongside her. Lifting its head, this second dragon also roared with fury. Suddenly all became clear. This was not the dusk dragon they had met earlier, but a day dragon – proud, strong and full of wrathful fire.

'Gods!' Husam exclaimed. The potential presence of a day dragon had never entered their thinking when they had discussed how they would strike.

The two dragons were beautiful, yet terrifying. Hunters normally killed them through stealth, but the element of surprise had been lost here. Husam knew it took a brave or foolish hunter to assault an alert and angry dragon.

In the light of the dawn dragon's glowing scales, every ridge and horn on the two creatures seemed sharper, larger and more deadly. The day dragon opened its jaws again, drawing in a deep breath. Its huge teeth gleamed ivory white for a moment before its head whipped forwards on its long neck, spewing a new jet of deadly flame across the meadow. It twisted its head from side to side, spraying the flames back and forth. The fire reflected in the great eyes of both dragons gave them an almost demonic appearance in the flickering light.

Although the flames fell short of the hunters, Husam was forced to turn away as the wave of heat struck him like a giant hammer. He dropped into a crouch, choking on the smoke and fumes. His hands rose automatically to protect his face as his shirt rapidly became hot against his back. He cried out in pain as he began to feel his skin cook. Billowing smoke and terrified yells filled the air and for a moment he thought he would bake where he crouched. Suddenly the punishing blast of heat stopped and Husam struggled upright in readiness to run.

A sudden movement caught his eye. It was Kasau. To Husam's amazement, even as the day dragon drew another breath, the hunter sprinted forwards through the writhing coils of smoke with a dragonbone blade in his hand. Those hunters not already running away were rooted where they stood. What did Kasau think he was doing? To attack two alert dragons alone and from a position of weakness was suicide.

A sudden roar from a different quarter struck such fear into Husam that his throat seemed to seize and his stomach knotted as he spun to face this new threat. The dusk dragon they thought had flown away was charging to attack the line of hunters from the right flank.

But if the dusk dragon is here, then what dragon did we see take off earlier? he thought. There were all together too many dragons. The attack had failed and if they were to escape with their lives, then they needed to run like they had never run before.

'Tembo! Run! Now!' he yelled, turning towards

the big man and grabbing his arm as he launched into a sprint. Tembo did not need any further encouragement. Together they pelted back across the meadow, reaching the stream in quick time.

As they slid down into the watercourse a huge shadow passed silently overhead, momentarily blotting out a large number of stars. Husam ducked his head and pulled Tembo down with him. An ear-piercing shriek suddenly split the air, bringing a wave of fear even more potent than that inspired by the roars of the three dragons.

'What on Areth is that?' Husam asked aloud. He looked back. He could not resist.

'That's Shadow. You don't want to mess with her,' said a girl's voice from no more than a few paces to his right. He whirled around. He could not see her through the smoke and darkness, but she sounded calm as she continued. 'I suggest you carry on running if you want to live. I would, if I were in your boots.'

At that moment the great shadow stooped. Husam whirled to watch in terrified fascination as it dropped like a stone from the sky onto the field from which he had just run. As it neared the ground he realised the shadow's target.

Kasau had almost reached the two waiting dragons when the deafening screech stopped him in his tracks. Confused, he looked around and saw the dusk dragon charging his line of hunters from the right. A flash of annoyance that none of the hunters had followed him in his attack caused him to curl his upper lip back in a snarl. He knew instantly, however, that the roaring dusk dragon had not made the unearthly screech. His eyes flicked upwards.

The dragonhunter dived to the right as Shadow dropped from the sky towards him like a giant falcon. Her massive talons missed him by a whisker, driving deep into the earth where he had been standing a split heartbeat before. As he rolled to his feet he swept the air above his body with his sword. The blade did not connect. Despite her size and heavily armoured hide, Shadow was wary of the dragonbone sword. She lunged, mouth gaping wide. Prudence stopped her short, just out of reach of the blade. For a moment, Kasau held her at bay and his mismatched eyes filled with fanatical zeal as he leaped into the offensive.

Husam stood entranced by the scene, with Tembo at his side. He felt duty bound to help his embattled leader, but fear and indecision kept him from moving. Kasau pressed forwards, forcing Shadow to hop back in a most ungainly fashion. The canny night dragon gave another dummy lunge as she did so, keeping the dragonhunter focused on her head and talons, whilst whipping her long tail around to strike from the side. If she had tried the tactic in the daytime, it was unlikely that it would have succeeded. But in the dying light offered by the remnants of the dawn dragon's fading glow, Kasau sensed the danger too late. The night dragon's tail smashed into him from the side with the weight and force of a falling tree.

The impact knocked him clear off his feet. Pain erupted in his chest as he fell and his sword flew from his grip, spinning end over end in a lazy arc. As he hit the ground, Kasau rolled, but he was not fast enough. More pain exploded like red fire as great talons pierced his thigh and stomach, pinning him to the ground. Instinctively he grabbed at the talons in an effort to pull himself free. They felt smooth and polished, like the marble pillars of the great temple in Mero where he had grown up, and equally as immovable, as he strained against the dragon's deadly hold. His strength was slipping away. He was soaked in his own blood. It was over. He knew it, but he could not accept it. Drifting smoke and the musky scent of the night dragon wafted over him. But it was the meaty breath and the great gaping jaws descending towards him that ignited his spirit to a final act of defiance. With a

249

shuddering gasp he drew his knife an instant before the great teeth struck.

Husam winced as Shadow pounced like an oversized cat. He saw the night dragon's talons impale Kasau, but to his amazement, despite the dragon's deadly strike he saw the dragonhunter reach to his hip and draw a dagger. What Kasau hoped to do with it, Husam could not begin to imagine, but before the dying hunter had a chance to raise the blade in anger, the dragon's jaws opened wide and bit him with the speed of a striking viper. Husam lowered his eyes quickly as the sickening sounds of Kasau's death were followed by a strange, rumbling growl of satisfaction from the dragon.

'Roughly translated, I believe that was dragon for "Mmm, crunchy!"' the girl's voice said calmly from the darkness. 'You'd better start running – she's got the taste for blood now.'

Husam was not about to argue with such obvious logic. He spun, but as he did so something hit him from behind with so much force that it picked him from his feet and threw him several paces through the air.

'Husam? Are you all right?' Tembo asked, racing to his friend's aid as he lay sprawled on the ground.

'I think so,' he gasped. His back still felt scorched and he could now smell that the hair on the back of his neck had been singed as well. 'Whatever hit me didn't hurt. Let's get out of here. This was a bad idea from the start.' His heart raced and his chest was heaving as he fought for breath. He did not want to say more. His mind seemed suddenly filled with strange pictures and sounds.

'No arguments with that here,' Tembo said quickly.

The big man hauled Husam to his feet and together they ran away into the valley as fast as they could. Had the light been better, or had Tembo paused to look his friend in the eyes before they ran, he might have thought twice about following his friend. It was not until the next morning that he was to discover the strange change in Husam. In the early misty light, as they stirred the ashes of their little campfire into life, a chill shot down Tembo's spine. It was startling. His friend's eyes were no longer their normal, azure blue – well, the right one was, but the left had changed. It was darker. So dark, it was almost purple.

Chapter Twenty
Journey

In the morning, swathes of blackened grass and odd fragmented remains of weapons were all that marked the dramatic events of the previous evening. Elian turned the dragonbone sword over and over in his hands as he considered what had happened. The sword looked identical to the one Kasau had carried, but that was impossible. Kasau and his hunting party were in Racafi, hundreds of leagues south of their position. It made no sense.

'Elian, I have a confession to make.' Aurora sounded embarrassed. Considering her normal superior tone, Elian was surprised to hear the penitent note in her voice.

'A confession, Ra?' he replied, looking up into his dragon's amber eyes. 'What sort of confession?'

'*We're not when we thought we were,*' she said cryptically.

Elian thought about that statement for a moment. It made no sense. 'What do you mean not *when?*' he asked. 'Surely you mean not *where?*'

There was a long pause in his mind. Elian could feel Ra's presence and a little of the emotion in her hesitation to answer.

'*The dragonhunters last night were the same group that we met in Racafi,*' she said slowly.

'Impossible!' Elian answered immediately. 'There's no way they could have got here in the couple of days since we escaped them.'

'*That would be true if it had been just a couple of days, but it hasn't. I pondered on it last night. It was Shadow who confirmed my suspicions. When we came through that last gateway I made a mistake that is likely to make our lives rather difficult for a while.*'

'What sort of mistake?' he asked, his mind replaying the last transfer.

'*Well when I explained the nature of the gateways and my ability to travel through them, I omitted one rather important fact. The relationship of time between our world and the one on the other side of the gateways is not linear.*'

'Not linear? I don't understand. What do you mean?'

'Whenever I go to the other world, I allow my dragon-sense to lead me to where and when I'm supposed to be,' Ra explained. 'However, when I come back I normally concentrate on emerging here in our world on the day after I left. On that last jump the strain of making the gateway took all my concentration, so I allowed my dragonsense to lead me. I expected to arrive here the day after we left Cemaria, but we didn't. We effectively spent three weeks in France. The dragonsense is a strange instinct. We dragons believe it is tied in with our destiny.'

'Three weeks! But I thought we had lots of time before the harvest moon. If you're right we only have ...'

'Just over six weeks to complete the quest,' Ra finished.

Elian nodded as he checked her calculation. This did not give them long to find the four orbs and get back to the Oracle. They would only have about ten days to track down each orb. Then a thought struck him.

'What if ... what if next time when you take us through the gateways you concentrate on bringing us back here before now? Go *back* in time! We could get the three weeks back,' he said excitedly.

'It can't be done,' Ra answered. 'When a point in time has passed, it's gone for ever. If I concentrate I can emerge an instant after we left, no matter how long we *spend on the other side. But I cannot take us into the past. The time is lost to us. I'm sorry.'*

Elian nodded. 'Well, we must trust your dragon-sense. If we're meant to succeed, we must still have time. We'll just have to make the most of every heartbeat from now on.'

'Then we must leave now. It's a long way to the enclave of the day dragons and I won't be able to open another gateway safely for some days yet.'

Elian did not need to ask why this was the case. He could still feel an echo of the mental fatigue he had experienced through the link when they came through the last gateway. He did not want to use the gateways again until Ra was recovered sufficiently. The dangers involved in getting stuck in the other world were too great.

To Elian's surprise, when he returned to the campsite, Nolita was ready to go. There was a glint of determination in her eyes, which before had only been displayed in denial of her destiny. Now she seemed set on continuing the quest.

They struck camp, taking care to ensure the fire was totally extinguished, but leaving the shelter intact. Assuming they found the orbs, they would be coming back this way, and having the framework in place would save them a lot of effort when they returned.

Buoyed by her triumph of the previous evening, Nolita tried again to approach Firestorm. She needed to ride a dragon to continue the quest. It made sense that she ride Firestorm, but no matter how hard she tried, it was as if an invisible force repelled her, making her stomach heave the moment she began to move in his direction. The nausea, frustration and fear brought tears to her eyes as she was forced to accept defeat.

Some heroine! she thought.

Firestorm crouched quietly on his haunches and watched her silent battle. It was frustrating to be so powerless, but he knew that anything he did would only make it harder for her.

Elian noted that the fear in her eyes looked as strong as ever as he helped her up onto Ra's back. He could see the muscles around her jaw bunching as she clenched her teeth together in an effort to control her emotions. Her face was deathly pale, but there were no protests today. She took her place silently and clamped her hands tightly around the pommel of the saddle.

Pell refused to abandon his solo quest for the night orb. He launched first on Shadow and as soon as she was airborne the night dragon turned eastwards. Pell gave them a final wave as Shadow powered upwards in the long climb over the mountains, and on towards the great continent of Isaa and the enclave of the night dragons.

In resignation, Kira shrugged and took the lead, leaping across the meadow on Fang. Elian adjusted the dragonhunter's sword that he had rigged across his back. Shadow had eaten the scabbard, so he had been forced to improvise. Since Elian had lost his sword to the dragonhunters during their first encounter it felt right to take this one in recompense.

'*Just you be careful with that thing*,' Ra warned, her voice disapproving. '*I don't want you inadvertently sticking me with it.*'

'I'll do my best,' Elian said, chuckling. 'Hold tight, Nolita. We're off.'

Once more, Elian delighted in the thrill of the take-off run and the feeling of wonder as the ground fell away beneath him. He sensed that Nolita was rigid with fear, but she did not cry out. He felt strangely proud of her. Her actions the previous evening – warning them of the approach of the dragonhunters through Firestorm – had shown considerable bravery.

Her calm account of the encounter had given cause for amusement. Firestorm confirmed through Ra that the conversations she had described were accurate. 'Mmm, crunchy!' Elian smiled to himself. Nolita had plenty of nerve when it came to facing

257

down people. Pell had not been able to see it, of course, but Elian suspected that Pell often only saw what he wanted to see.

The morning mist was thin. Above the murky layer the sky was totally clear of cloud. The white-capped mountains, shouldering into the vast ocean of blue, made for breathtaking views. The wind had dropped overnight, so the turbulence of the previous day was no longer a cause for concern. Today the air was smooth, clear and crisp. Perfect, Elian thought. If Nolita could just relax when it's like this, she might learn to enjoy flying.

They turned southwards and westwards, away from the mountains and towards the lowlands that predominated the landmass between here and the sea. They would have to cross the water back into northern Racafi, before heading further south and westwards towards the far western coast where the continent met the ocean. Firestorm had told them that the enclave of the day dragons was located in great caves to be found in the side of one of two ancient volcanoes near the coast. The volcanoes had been extinct for many hundreds of years, leaving them as perfect homes for large groups of dragons. Local human population was sparse, so the dragons were able to hunt the lands nearby with little worry of accidentally eating livestock or domesticated animals.

Even on dragonback it would take at least five days to cover the distance to the enclave. They cruised at no more than a thousand spans above the ground, keeping within relatively warm air. As the sun climbed, the temperature warmed significantly, allowing them to climb a little higher without getting too cold. Despite the smooth ride and the pleasant temperatures, Nolita remained rigid in the saddle throughout the morning.

They landed for a short break in the middle of the day to take lunch. By the time they began their descent the morning mist had long since burned off, leaving the countryside spread beneath them like a giant patchwork quilt of many colours. In some places great squares of land had been tilled and set to crops. In others, the contrasting greens of woodland, pasture and swampy marshlands offered many pleasant patterns. They landed where a meadow met a stand of trees. There was no visible sign of human habitation in sight. When Elian helped Nolita down from Ra's back, she was stiff and silent. On setting foot on solid ground, she was quick to move away from the dragons, sit down and wash her hands with water from her drinking bottle.

Elian collected some deadwood from amongst the trees, while Kira prepared food. Once they had an appropriate amount of kindling, she set about building the fire and cooked them a meal. There was still plenty of mutton left from the previous evening, so Elian and Kira ate heartily in preparation for another long flight in the afternoon.

Nolita picked at the food, her complexion almost grey despite the bright sun. She said little throughout the meal, her eyes appearing distant as Elian and Kira chatted about the quest, the incident with the dragonhunters and the journey ahead. But when it was time to move on she remounted Ra without any fuss and her jaw set in a determined line as she climbed back into the saddle. She was clearly still terrified, but she did it anyway.

The afternoon's flight was every bit as smooth and pleasant as the one they had made in the morning. When the coast of the Pascian Sea appeared ahead of them in the late afternoon, Ra informed Elian that they would land. To continue further meant flying through the night in order to make landfall on the far shore. Having ridden bareback behind his saddle all day, Elian was more than happy with that decision. His backside was numb after the long trip. A dull throbbing pulsed through his lower back, and the muscles in his groin had long since crossed the point of discomfort into active pain.

For Nolita the day had been a waking nightmare. She spent the entire time forcing her eyes to focus on the back of Aurora's head and telling herself over and over not to look down. Without the security of Elian's arms around her, she felt sure she would have fainted and fallen to her death.

They landed on the beach near a small village. As soon as the riders had dismounted, the dragons were quick to dive into the surf. The local children ran out in a great gaggle to watch in delight as the three enormous dragons proceeded to cavort in the water. Great fountains of spray exploded into the air as they leaped and plunged, rolling and diving with surprising speed.

Elian found himself amused by Aurora's excesses in the water. For all her regal tones and superior manner at times he was pleased to discover that she was not beyond having some fun. For an instant he felt he could see past her imperious air, her strange abilities and her physical size and shape, and the sight of her behaving like a happy child, playing with water, made her seem a little more human.

Nolita did not see the dragons playing. She could hear the thunderous splashes, but ignored them. The moment she dismounted she turned her back on the dragons and staggered quickly across the sand towards the nearest cottages, thankful that today's flight was finally over. Her knees were weak with relief and the desire to wash her hands was overwhelming. The sea was the nearest source of water, but her need to get away from the dragons was even stronger than her need to wash.

The welcome from the villagers was warm. Nolita was led to a washroom and later the three companions were given food and lodging for the night, with nothing asked in return except stories from their travels. With all that had happened over the past week, Elian and Kira found no difficulty in entertaining the crowd, though Nolita made her excuses and sat in silence.

The next day the entire village came out to watch them depart. After a good night's sleep in a real bed, even Nolita managed a stiff wave as they powered up into the bright morning sky and turned south and west across the seemingly endless expanse of water. The flight across the sea was without incident, as were the next two days as they crossed the edge of the great North Racafian Desert. The heart of the vast desert was to the east of their track, for which they were all grateful. The desert was renowned to be one of the most hostile places on Areth. Even dragons hesitated to cross the centre of the desert, unless dire need drove them.

When the fifth day dawned, there was an undercurrent of excitement and anticipation. If all went well, this would be the last leg of their journey to the day dragon enclave. As they shared a modest breakfast, Nolita looked nervous, but there was a sense of energy about her that had been lacking on previous mornings.

Shortly after sunrise they took to the air. The cloudless early morning sky promised another beautiful day for flying, but it did not remain that way for long. They had been flying for no more than an hour before the first isolated cumulus clouds began to form, mushrooming rapidly into towering columns with great cauliflower heads. They looked bright and clean, with hard edges that could almost have been solid.

The storm clouds continued to grow throughout the morning until the great pillars of cloud hit their natural ceiling and the tops began to dissipate into enormous anvil-shapes. The dragons were forced to make long diversions in order to keep a safe distance away. Occasional rumbles of thunder gave Nolita something new to be frightened about. Was the threat from fiery bolts of lightning greater when up in the sky than it was on the ground? She did not ask Elian if he knew, as she suspected she did not want to know the answer. The reason for the dragons' caution became apparent when they began to encounter turbulent air several leagues from the edges of the clouds.

Nolita had begun to relax into the saddle a little during the past few days, but the first of the stomach-churning lurches had her white-knuckled and bolt upright in an instant. The mind-numbing fear that she had experienced during the turbulent flight to the Oracle's cave smashed through her mind again with terrible force. Elian tensed behind her, which did not help. If he was scared, then she knew her fear was not irrational. The following two hours were uncomfortable and terrifying beyond belief.

Periods of several minutes at a time where the air was smooth were followed by spells when the air seemed alive with currents almost actively intent on bouncing the riders from the dragons' backs. If time had not been pressing the riders would have landed and waited out the difficult conditions, but they knew they could not afford to waste a moment. The faster they obtained the day orb, the more time they would have to solve the rest of the riddles.

'Firestorm is taking the lead. He says he can see

our destination,' Elian said suddenly, his voice making Nolita jump.

She did not respond. She couldn't. Her mouth opened, but nothing came out. Her brain felt scrambled.

They began to descend. There were some large gaps between the clouds, but as Firestorm powered ahead, Nolita could see that he was not heading for one of them. The day dragon entered a shallow dive and turned towards a narrow slot between two shelving layers of cloud. The ground visible through the narrow gap looked to be in deep shadow, but as they raced downwards, almost skimming the surface of the cloud layer beneath them, they soon discovered it was not shadow alone that made the ground appear dark.

The rain began abruptly. Large warning spots were followed by a wall of pounding water-droplets that carried the sting of a bee with every impact. Nolita might have cried out with shock and pain, but instead she found herself closing her mouth tightly and holding her breath as they drove ever faster into the ocean of biting water-darts. The saddle became slick beneath her and she clung with a growing sense of panic to the pommel as the wind caused Ra to buck and roll beneath her.

She could no longer see ahead. Initially she tried

to squint, but it was useless. The raindrops were so big and densely packed that they blurred her vision and stung her eyes.

'*Hold on. We're nearly out of this.*' Firestorm's voice in her head was a lifeline. She had never thought to be glad to have the dragon speak to her, but his voice lifted her spirit. '*Another few heartbeats and we'll be clear.*'

As suddenly as it started, the stinging rain stopped. The vicious turbulence also eased to a less frantic tempo and Nolita cautiously cracked open her eyes. Ahead was a sight that set her pulse racing even faster. The broad base of a huge volcano loomed in front of them, its crown lost in clouds. Firestorm began to adjust his course and Nolita saw the opening ahead – a vast gash in the mountainside that looked as if a giant had stabbed it with some weapon of gargantuan proportion.

Nolita did not need Firestorm to tell her they had arrived at the day dragon enclave.

Chapter Twenty-One
Day Dragon Enclave

'Welcome, dragonriders. I am Barnabas, eldest of the day dragonriders at the enclave. Come. Join us. It's almost time to eat and I'm sure you must be ready for a good meal. My dragon tells me you have come directly from the Oracle's cave.'

The young riders eyed Barnabas with wonder. He was tall and slim, with long white hair tied back in a ponytail. His neat, short-cropped white beard contrasted with an impressive moustache, long and drooping. His eyes were the brightest of blues, sparkling with life and merriment from his lined face. Despite his obvious age he walked like one twenty rotations his junior, and his bright eyes and warm smile soon put the three companions at ease.

'Thank you, sir,' Elian responded. 'I'm Elian and this is Kira and Nolita. We appreciate your welcome, but we're here on an urgent quest. Our duty to the Oracle must come first.'

Barnabas nodded. 'Of course,' he said. 'I fully understand. However, I'm already aware of the nature of your quest. A crystal orb formed on the sacred plinth in the Sun's Steps chamber not two weeks ago. We're not ignorant as to its significance. When my dragon, Sharphorn, and I visited the Oracle many years ago we were tasked with testing the worthiness of the rider who would come to our enclave seeking such an orb. We have spent much time over the years researching previous orb quests, so, as you can imagine, we've been awaiting your arrival these last few days with a certain amount of anticipation. I must admit, though, I'm a little confused. In the past, four riders have undertaken this quest. Where is the fourth member of your party?'

Elian exchanged glances with Kira.

'Pell rides a night dragon, sir,' Kira said quickly. 'He didn't come because he was worried about stirring up old troubles between the day and night enclaves.'

Barnabas pursed his lips into a tight line. 'It's sad that such misunderstandings are still spread by members of the night dragon enclave. We have no love for the night dragons and their riders, it's true, but we would never seek to hinder any dragon or rider who is seeking to fulfil his life's destiny. To do so would be to deny all that we are. Where is he?'

'He's gone to his enclave to look for the night orb, sir,' Elian replied.

'Then the urgency of your mission is greater than you know,' Barnabas said gravely. 'If the leaders of the night dragon enclave discover that the Great Quest has begun again, they will do everything in their power to prevent you from achieving your goal. Members of the night dragon enclave caused the previous quests to fail. Come. We shall discuss this further over some food. You will face the first part of your quest at midday tomorrow, so you would do well to eat and rest now. You will need all your strength over the coming days. Which of you is Firestorm's rider?'

'I am, sir,' Nolita replied softly, her face still pale after the terrifying flight.

Barnabas raised an eyebrow in mild surprise, but said nothing. He acknowledged Nolita with a slight nod and turned to lead the way into a labyrinth of caves.

The young riders quickly lost track of the way as they zigzagged through numerous caverns and tunnels, which all looked the same. But the old man led the way without hesitation, as if their path were marked with clear signs.

'*Do not worry, Elian,*' Ra assured him. '*All is well. All say Barnabas is an honourable dragonrider. He and the others of this enclave will want us to succeed in our quest. You need fear no one while you are here.*'

'*That's good to know, Ra,*' Elian replied. '*Thank you. Enjoy your rest. I suspect we'll need your strength to take us through a gateway back to the Oracle if we're to stand a chance of getting all four orbs in time.*'

'*I'll be ready,*' Ra assured him. '*It all depends on Nolita now. If she cannot gain the first orb, then we will fail before we begin. Listen carefully to Barnabas's words. He is considered wise even by dragon standards.*'

High praise indeed from a dragon, Elian mused – particularly from one with such strong notions of dragon superiority. The old man looked the part of the wise old dragonrider, but appearances could prove deceptive. Nolita was a prime example.

He automatically turned to look at her and she met his eyes with an expression full of fear and distrust. He gave her an encouraging smile, but when Nolita's expression did not change, he looked away hurriedly. The last thing he wanted was to make matters worse. If their interpretation of the Oracle's words were correct, then something was going to happen here that would test her bravery. Nolita needed all the encouragement that he and Kira could give.

Please let it be enough, he prayed silently.

Barnabas led them to a huge underground hall. Long lines of tables were set with cutlery, ready for a meal. A few men and women were already taking their places as a huge gong was rung to announce the meal. The three young riders were led to a special table set aside from the main lines.

'Please, take a seat,' Barnabas urged them. 'Anywhere at the table will be fine. Other, senior riders will join us shortly.'

As if on cue, a stream of riders poured into the huge dining hall from every entrance. The tables filled rapidly, including theirs. When all the places were taken, Barnabas got to his feet and the assembled riders fell silent. With simple dignity he offered a short prayer of thanks to the Creator for the food they were about to eat and the diners muttered 'We agree'. There was a momentary silence as Barnabas took his seat. No sooner had he sat down, however, than lines of serving men and women entered bearing platters of steaming food and the buzz of animated conversation and laughter built in a rapid crescendo.

Elian could barely contain his excitement at being in the presence of so many experienced dragonriders. He had a myriad of questions about flying and about what it meant to be a part of the dragonrider community, but he was desperate not to show his ignorance in such revered company. As he struggled to frame a worthy question, he caught sight of Nolita out of the corner of his eye. She had chosen a seat at the end corner of the table, as far from the centre of conversation as possible. Her head was down and she was pushing at her food with a fork. Elian felt a rush of sympathy for her as he tried to imagine what was going through her mind.

Come on, Nolita, he thought, willing her to be strong. Hold yourself together. You've come too far to fall apart now.

Nolita had never felt so wretched. Feeling so alone, like a solitary island in the midst of a sea of riders, rated as the worst moment of her life. Her fears had always set her apart – yet, curiously, the feeling of isolation that gripped her now was not the sort of fear with which she was familiar. For once the gut-twisting terror that so often ruled her life was not the issue. This fear was more of a deep worry – a concern that even if she did *attain the orb* and *vanquish the fears* she still might never feel at home with these people.

A gentle touch on her arm made her jump. The rider next to her was a woman of middle years. She had strong, angular features and was sitting proud and straight in her chair.

'Are you all right?' the woman asked.

'I'll be fine,' Nolita mumbled. 'Thank you, anyway.'

'Is it the fears?' she whispered.

Nolita's eyes snapped up to look at her. What did she know? Who had told her? Nolita glanced swiftly around the table for Elian and Kira to see if she could identify which of them had told tales behind her back.

'What do you mean?' Nolita asked quietly, her tone wary as she brought her attention back to meet the woman's sympathetic gaze.

'The trial – the test of bravery required to claim the orb,' the woman answered. 'I hear you've come on the Great Quest. You are Firestorm's rider, aren't you? If so, then I salute you. I wouldn't like to have to face my worst fears. I don't think I'd fare very well. I don't blame you for being daunted. It's a huge responsibility. Particularly this time, as failure will mean the end of dragonkind as we know it.'

'Thanks for the reminder,' Nolita said sourly, though no sooner had the bitter words passed her lips than she regretted them. This woman knew something about the orb and how she was supposed to get it. Any information she had might be critical.

'Sorry! I didn't mean to make it worse,' the woman rider said quickly, her hand flying to her mouth. 'That last bit slipped out before I could stop it. I just wanted to say that everyone here is willing you to succeed. I apologise if it didn't come out the right way.'

'Forget it,' Nolita replied, forcing a wan smile. 'No harm done. Do you know anything about the trial? Is it a secret, or is there anything I can do to prepare?'

'How can anyone prepare against coming face to face with their worst nightmare? All you can do is steel your heart and do your best when the time comes. I'll be there. We all will, though we won't experience what you will. All we'll see is your success or failure. I pray it will be the former.'

'Thank you. Do you know when the trial will happen?' Nolita asked nervously.

'Tomorrow at noon in the Chamber of the Sun's Steps, but they'll have to do an assessment of your fears tonight in order to give the dragons a chance to prepare.'

'They?' Nolita did not like what she was hearing. 'Who are *they*? And what are the dragons going to prepare?'

'If you don't know yet, then it's not my place to tell you,' the woman answered, looking around furtively as she realised she might have said too much. 'Don't worry, dragonrider. I'm sure you'll do fine.'

That's easy for you to say, Nolita thought, clenching her teeth to prevent an outburst she knew she would regret later. You won't have to face the dreaded trial.

For the rest of the meal she sat in silence. The isolation she had felt when she first sat down became more complete, yet more bearable. Her thoughts and feelings swung wildly. One moment she felt a sensation of contentment in her solitude and the next she wallowed in the loneliness and vulnerability associated with treading her own path.

Did she want to be a part of this society? Yes . . . and no. She did not know. There were too many factors to consider. To be a dragonrider like these folk meant riding regularly on a dragon for the rest of her life. The thought made her stomach churn. Yet, like it or not, she was bonded to one of the creatures. There was no escape, save through death. She had briefly considered suicide after running away from home, but had soon decided she was not ready to give up on life so easily.

The meal ended after what seemed to her like

an eternity. Barnabas rose from his seat, and placed a gentle hand on her shoulder. 'Come,' he said, 'follow me.' Amidst the confusion of the after-dinner rush for the doors he began to lead her across the hall to one of the doorways on the other side.

'Wait! We want to come too.'

The voice was Kira's. Nolita's heart leaped. Once again her companions were sticking by her. They never gave up.

'That's not permitted. Go with Leto. He will see you to the guest rooms,' Barnabas replied, his voice stern.

'Why can't we come?' Elian asked. 'There'll be others there, won't there? We won't interfere. We just want to support our friend.'

'There is a strict protocol involved with the orb. I dare not break it. To gain the orb, Nolita must prove herself worthy. This is her task. If she's successful, then your turn to face trials will come soon enough, dawn dragonrider. Go. Your friend will be fine. You have my word that no harm will come to her before the trial of bravery tomorrow.'

'And at the trial? What about at the trial? Will you guarantee her safety then as well?' Kira asked, her eyebrows knitted together in a deep frown.

Barnabas met her frown with an even expression. 'The trial should not involve grave physical danger, but Nolita's safety will depend on the nature of her deepest fears. Once the trial begins, the outcome will be dictated by her strength of mind.'

'Then she'll pass it easily,' Elian said firmly. 'Don't worry. You'll do it, Nolita,' he added, looking her in the eyes. 'You're stronger than you think.'

Nolita gave a weak smile in return, but held her silence. She did not feel strong. She felt nervous and her knees felt so wobbly that they might give way at any moment. Her two companions gave a final wave and turned to follow their guide. Barnabas placed his hand gently on her shoulder and steered her across the hall and out into the maze of tunnels.

The assessment did not take long. She stood quaking in the middle of a large chamber with Barnabas at her side while three blue day dragons regarded her with baleful stares. Mingled with the usual feelings of fear and revulsion, which she struggled to control, there was a tingling sensation inside her skull, but yet she felt no pain. Were the dragons looking into her mind? Firestorm could do that, but his presence in her mind was some-thing tangible. This was strange, as she could not identify another consciousness.

A minute passed in silence before the dragons turned and looked at one another. The tingling stopped and Barnabas squeezed her shoulder.

'All done,' he said kindly.

'That's it?'

'They have what they need from you,' he said. 'They'll assess Firestorm separately.'

'Firestorm?'

'Yes,' he said, smiling in his gentle way. 'You will not be alone. Did you think attaining the orb was just your responsibility? You seek a dragon orb. Both dragon and rider must be found worthy to claim it. Come. I'll take you to your room now and you can get some rest. I know you're nervous, but try to get what sleep you can.'

Chapter Twenty-Two
A Test of Bravery

A vast cave within the volcano formed the Chamber of the Sun's Steps. Enormous shelves of rock, many times the height of a man, climbed from the centre of the cave with remarkable regularity to the opening at the upper end. It was easy to see why they were referred to as steps, though one would have to be a giant, far larger even than a dragon, to make use of them.

With a bare few minutes until midday, Nolita stepped from an entrance on one side of the giant cave. As she entered, she saw Firestorm appear through a much larger entrance diagonally across to her right, on the far side of the chamber. Nolita's heart seemed to pause in her chest as she saw the dragon move into the centre of the cave floor. Just the sight of him made her stomach begin to knot.

Gods! she thought. How am I going to get through this?

'*I will be with you,*' Firestorm said firmly. '*We will get through it together. Do not panic. I know how hard it is for you to accept that you are my rider, Nolita. But nothing you say or do can change that. I know you are frightened of me, but try to see past that today. I'm sure we will both make our companions proud.*'

Although brave and full of confidence, the dragon's words brought little comfort.

Barnabas was waiting for them. On a vast shelf of rock to one side of the great cave, all the dragon-riders presently staying at the enclave were standing in orderly lines. If Elian and Kira were among them, Nolita could not pick them out. On the other side of the cave, crouching on tiers, were a host of day dragons. Despite herself, Nolita could not suppress a shudder at the sight of them. Aurora and Longfang were in prime position on the lowest tier, their colours standing out against the lines of blue dragons.

Nolita and Firestorm walked forwards into the chamber until they were facing one another about forty paces apart in the centre of the great cave. Barnabas raised his hands in a gesture to stop them where they were. He then bowed to each of them in turn. Firestorm dipped his head upon his long neck to approximate the motion of a return bow and Nolita followed his lead by giving an awkward bow of her own.

'In a few heartbeats your trial will begin,' Barnabas announced in a strong, clear voice. 'Last night the Council of Senior Dragons looked deep into your minds to find that which you fear most in this world, or any other. When the sun's rays strike the first step, the Council will seek to test you, projecting what you most fear into your mind so that you are forced to confront it. The experience will feel very real, but will not be shared by anyone else present. Your joint objective is to overcome your fears and retrieve the orb. As part of your test the plinth on which it rests has been moved to the peak of the sister volcano a few miles to the south of here. It is on the most southerly rim of the peak. You will find it clearly visible. Good luck.'

He bowed again, and stepped briskly away towards the long lines of fascinated riders. It took a moment for the full implications of the instructions to filter into Nolita's conscious thoughts. The orb was on the peak of a neighbouring mountain. The only way she could get there was . . .

She looked at her huge blue dragon and her stomach convulsed. Firestorm had been fitted with a dragon saddle. It was as if the jaws of a huge trap had just sprung shut around her. She would have to ride him to retrieve the orb – ride him on her own.

Somehow she restrained herself from being sick on the spot, but she knew that one more convulsion would see her heaving what little food she had managed to eat onto the rocky floor of the cave.

'Peace, Nolita. Be calm. You have ridden on Aurora. Riding on my back will be no different. The sister peak is no more than a few minutes away. It will be over before you realise it.'

Firestorm's attempt to play down the significance of what was being asked of her did not work.

'No different!' she thought back, her anger momentarily swamping her fear with its burning power. *'No different! Of course it'll be different. When I rode Ra, Elian was behind me. This time I'll be alone – alone on you! Don't tell me there's no difference between riding Ra and riding you, because you feel it as much as I do. I know you do. I feel your thoughts. I feel your . . .'* Nolita paused. The shock of what she could feel emanating through the mental link with the dragon sent her mind spiralling into confusion. *'. . . fear! Oh, gods, what fear! But that's not . . . I don't understand.'*

A sudden beam of light stabbed down from the roof of the chamber, striking the lowest step like a great golden spear. Even with the backdrop of the open sky at the end of the cave, the shaft of light seemed a solid column of amber fire. It was beautiful, yet it was also terrifying. Nolita knew that this must be the signal for the beginning of her trial.

She looked around nervously, half expecting to see hordes of screaming monsters materialising in every corner. She took a deep, shuddering breath and held it for a moment. Nothing. She expelled her breath silently, not wishing to make any noise in case it triggered something horrible around her.

'Everyone fears something, Nolita. It is ironic that you embodied my fears, as I have embodied yours. I have lived in fear ever since I met you, for you were not what I expected. It is quite likely that our fears have fed on each other, as our bond allows emotion to pass between us.'

Nolita turned and faced Firestorm, looking him properly in the eyes for the first time. The pain and hurt there were clear to see. The thought that she had been the cause of that pain touched her deep inside. It did not lessen her fear of him, but a tiny piece of understanding seemed to click into place within her.

'Are you telling me that some of my fear isn't mine at all?' she asked.

'I would say that is likely, yes.'

'But what can you possibly find to be frightened of

in me?' she asked, wondering if he was somehow making it up to make her feel better.

'*I fear that you will not find me worthy of acceptance,'* Firestorm replied, his mental voice suddenly timid as he opened his heart to her. '*I fear rejection. I fear that other dragons will see me and say, "Look, there's Firestorm – the dragon so pathetic his rider would not acknowledge their bond."'*

'*But that's not—'*

'*Not true,'* he interrupted. '*Not the reason you cannot be my rider. Yes, I know. I know it as you know it. I understand your fear, Nolita. I taste it in my mind constantly. How could I not come to understand it? But look around you, Nolita. Do you think the others here understand it? Can you see why my fears are every bit as valid as yours?'*

Nolita looked around at the lines of watching dragonriders, and then turned to look at the ranks of dragons. She shuddered. A week ago she would have fainted under the scrutiny of even one pair of those huge, lurking beasts' eyes. Since spending a week in the presence of dragons she realised it would take more than a dragon's stare to produce such a response in her again.

'*I think I understand,'* she admitted slowly. '*What do you think they see, though?'*

'*I believe they see us both standing tall and facing*

our fears without flinching,' Firestorm replied. '*If you were to climb on my back now and let me carry you up to collect the orb, then they would likely consider us heroic, for we would have achieved something that many of them do not wish to attempt.*'

'So this is the test? All I have to do is ride you to collect the orb?' Nolita asked.

'*It appears that by doing so you will have faced your deepest fear. That is what the test demands.*'

'And you? Where is the test for you in that?' she demanded, feeling very much that she was getting the worst of this test.

'*I face the possibility that you will baulk and walk away. My shame amongst my peers will then live with me for ever.*' Firestorm paused for a moment to let his words sink in. '*I know how difficult this is for you, Nolita, but I will not beg you. This is your choice. Will you come with me and collect the first orb? It is waiting for us.*'

The churning in her stomach intensified as she forced herself to consider climbing into the waiting saddle. The silence in the great cavern was deafening. She closed her eyes and tried to remember the feeling of bravery that the Oracle had momentarily inspired in her heart. If she failed, the Oracle would die. She did not want to be responsible for killing the one who had given her hope. If she climbed into the saddle and let Firestorm carry her up to the orb, her companions would be ecstatic. The image of their response was vivid in her mind's eye. She would be a heroine worthy of the tales she had so loved as a little girl. How hard could it be?

Nolita drew in a deep breath through her nose and expelled it through her mouth. She inhaled another and then took a step forwards. No sooner had she made that first step than a deep rumble shook the chamber. Was the volcano about to erupt? Was it an earthquake? The floor of the chamber ahead of her bucked and heaved before crumbling and dropping away. Her breath caught in her throat and she dropped to one knee for stability as she found herself facing a narrow bridge of rock that spanned an abyss of immeasurable depth between her and Firestorm. There was no way around. The walls to either side were sheer, offering no alternative route.

'*Don't look down!*' Firestorm said quickly.

'*Too late,*' Nolita replied, her head spinning as she fought to control her breathing. Sweat broke out on her forehead and every muscle in her body tightened. It's not real, she told herself. It can't be. The other dragons and dragonriders would have reacted if it was real. There would have been panic.

'*Look at me, Nolita,*' Firestorm said, keeping his

tone calm and supportive. '*Concentrate on me. Treat everything else here as illusion. This is a test, but the Oracle wants you to succeed. It doesn't want to harm you. You felt that in your encounter. Barnabas and the dragons don't want to hurt you either. You know it's true. Come on! Focus. You can do it. I believe in you.*'

'It's so narrow,' she thought back, as she took in the yawning depths to either side of her. The bridge was not even a full pace wide and although it was formed of rock, it did not look strong enough to support her weight.

'*It's not real,*' Firestorm assured her. '*The cavern is as it was. The ground beneath your feet is solid.*'

She clenched her fingers into fists, feeling the slickness of sweat on her palms. He was right. She knew it, but her mind could not accept it over the evidence of her eyes. What would happen if she were to fall off the bridge, or ignore it altogether and step off the cliff?

'*Don't do that,*' Firestorm warned. '*The illusions created by dragons can feel very real. Just look at me and concentrate on walking across the bridge.*'

'*All right. I'll do my best.*'

Nolita stood up slowly and looked ahead at Firestorm. His appearance had changed. He looked to be almost leering at her. Was that a hint of red in his eyes? Had his horns grown longer? His lips were drawn back to reveal a toothy grin that looked distinctly evil. She drew in a deep breath and closed her eyes for a moment to see if she could dispel the image. She opened her eyes. If anything, Firestorm looked even more evil than before.

'It's all illusion,' she said aloud. 'It's not real. I can do this. I am strong enough.'

With grim determination she took a step forwards onto the narrow span of rock. It held her weight. She took another. The bridge shuddered and there was a horrible sound of grating rock, but it held. Her stomach was knotted so tight that it felt as if she would never be able to eat again. Another step forwards. Right foot in front of left. Left in front of right. Step by step she moved across the span until she reached the mid point. Left in front of right – suddenly the rock under her right foot crumbled and she stepped forwards quickly as a section of the bridge began to fall away behind her.

'*Run!*' Firestorm urged. '*Don't think. Just run!*'

A crack appeared a pace ahead of her and she leaped forwards, entering a madcap sprint across the rest of the span. As she ran the bridge continued to crumble away behind her, the segments falling silently into the black void. Ahead of her the dragon got to his feet, his jaws opening wide in anticipation of her arrival on his side of the abyss. Nolita skidded to a momentary halt. Which was the better end – to fall into the abyss, or be eaten by the waiting beast?

'*No! Don't stop, Nolita. Keep going!*' Firestorm urged.

For the first time, Nolita felt trust and love flooding through the bond. He was right. This was the test. He was not the evil creature she could see. She had felt his pride when she had warned him of the dragonhunters. If she did as he said, she would feel his pride again. It felt good to have someone proud of her. The apparition before her was horrible – enormous and terrifying beyond belief, but somehow she closed her mind to it and sprinted forwards again. For a moment she felt she was not going to make it. The collapsing sections behind her cracked and fell with increasing pace, but with a final surge she launched into a flying leap that carried her across to the far side even as the bridge fell away beneath her.

As she landed, she fell and rolled forwards until she was directly beneath the slavering jaws of the beast. Her heart nearly froze in her chest, but the beast made no move to attack, so she climbed carefully back to her feet.

'*Well done, Nolita,*' Firestorm said, his proud voice filling her with warmth. It felt good. She could do this. It was possible. Ignoring his appearance, she moved towards Firestorm's foreleg. In her mind she tried to imagine that she was about to climb onto Aurora's back as she had done every day for the past five days. She pictured Elian climbing into position behind her and his steadying hands on her waist. It was a comforting image, but it shattered when her fingers touched Firestorm's scales.

The sensation she felt as she touched him for the first time sent a shock through her body. Her instinctive reaction was to pull back as if burned. This was nothing like touching Aurora. The sensation was a world apart, as if her fingertips were touching an extension of her own body. Her fingers somehow joined with the dragon in a way that felt astonishingly intimate.

Her instinct was to turn and run. If she went through with this, she would have to face it every day. To face *this* every day? It was too much for them to ask of her. Shudders of horror ripped through her body. She began to turn with the intention of escaping as fast as she could, but as she did so, the Oracle's voice seemed to whisper in her ear. Its words froze her in place as it echoed through her mind. '*Attain ye the orb; vanquish the fears. Attain ye the orb; vanquish the fears. Attain ye . . .*'

She did not want to let the Oracle down. The Oracle had given her hope. It would die without her help. Repeating this over and over in her head, Nolita regained her focus. With gritted teeth she placed her hand on Firestorm's side and with swift, unthinking movements, she climbed his foreleg and swung her body up into the saddle. She gripped the pommel, her palms slick with sweat as another convulsive shudder rippled through her body.

'Take us out of here, Firestorm,' she shouted, her voice reverberating in the huge cavern. 'We've got an orb to find.'

Firestorm did not need telling twice. He let out a roar of triumph and in two quick paces was airborne, his joy at his rider's courage lending his wings extraordinary power. As they soared into the air and climbed through the glorious golden pillar of light, the cavern filled with the cheers of the gathered riders and the approving roars of the assembled dragons.

The view as they emerged from the mouth of the gigantic cavern was extraordinary. They were inside the crater of the volcano, surrounded on all sides by vertical walls of rock. Below them, the crater's floor was punctuated with pockets of greenery and pools of water. The very centre was effectively a shallow lake, its water sparkling like the surface of a giant jewel in the midday sun. Nolita had never seen anything like it before and, surrounded by the walls of rock, she forgot about heights as Firestorm circled upwards to escape the volcano's throat for the open sky beyond.

When they reached the rim of the crater, the sister peak became apparent immediately. It was a few leagues south and west of the peak containing the day dragon enclave. Firestorm flew towards it at speed to minimise the time in the air for his rider.

After the storms of the previous day, the sky looked almost washed clean of cloud. A few fair-weather cumulous clouds bumbled along in the distance, widely scattered and showing no signs of growth. Aside from a very occasional light bump, the air aloft was smooth and the breeze light.

Once free from the top of the first volcano, however, Nolita's fear returned in force. The side of the volcano dropped away beneath her so far that at the base leagues below, individual trees were no longer distinguishable. Woodland had become a carpet in another shade of green. She was alone on a dragon's back, far, far above the ground. Her fingers clamped even more tightly around the pommel of the saddle, her knuckles bright white with the effort. Her head started to spin with dizziness and her heart pounded as she fought to remain conscious.

'Don't look down. Don't look down. Don't look . . .' she panted, frantically trying to regain control.

'*I will not let you die, Nolita. If you fall, I will catch you.*'

Nolita clung to Firestorm's words – not for comfort, but because at this moment she could think of nothing worse than to have the dragon's talons, or jaws, pluck her from the air.

Must not faint, she thought. Not far to go. Focus on the peak. Look for the orb. Stay in control.

Somehow she fought down the panic attack, ruthlessly suppressing her natural instinct to pass out. The ground was rising towards them again, and as their height reduced, her panic lessened. She saw the flash of light on the southernmost edge of the rim long before she saw anything in detail.

'Did you see that?' she called aloud.

'*Yes, Nolita,*' he replied. '*It was very bright. We'll be there in just a moment or two.*'

They swooped in to land with Nolita holding her breath. The drop to either side of the rim appeared horrific, but the dragon landed lightly and without hesitation.

As soon as Firestorm had settled, Nolita unlocked her fingers from the pommel and slid down his side. She hurried several paces from the dragon and sat down. Suddenly it was all too much; the effects of her wild emotional swings caught up, her stomach convulsed and she vomited.

'*Are you all right?*' Firestorm's voice in her head was filled with concern.

'A lot better now,' she replied aloud with a laugh that held a note of hysteria. She wiped her mouth with the back of her hand. 'Give me a minute and I'll be fine.'

Chapter Twenty-Three
The First Orb

Nolita's head was spinning. Her chest felt tight with a combination of raging emotions, together with the physical after-effects of the flying and her sickness. With her eyes closed and her head in her hands, the trial of bravery she'd been through so far began to blur into a dreamlike montage of images, yet she did not need to pinch herself to know that it had been real.

She opened her eyes and eased herself gently to her feet. The orb was nearby, mounted on a plinth of solid metal that must have been put there to prevent it from being damaged. Nolita approached it cautiously, a sudden premonition prickling her senses.

The orb was a little larger than an apple and looked to be a perfectly spherical piece of hollow crystal. It was beautiful, refracting multicoloured rainbows of colour in the sunlight, but at the same time it looked disappointingly ordinary. How could recovering this pretty bauble help to save the Oracle? Did it have special powers? She reached out her hand towards it, but hesitated. Her fingers hovered for a moment above the surface of the crystal and then she withdrew them. This was what she had undergone the trial to obtain. What was she waiting for?

'*What is it, Nolita? Is something the matter?*'

'I'm not sure, Firestorm,' she replied aloud, grateful to have a reason to voice her misgivings. 'It's probably my imagination, but I've got a weird feeling something's not right here. I think there's something about the orb that Barnabas hasn't told us. Do you think this could be another part of the trial?'

Firestorm concentrated for a moment. Nolita could feel him reaching out with his mind.

'*I sense nothing from the orb. As far as I can tell, there's no danger here,*' he said, giving what Nolita interpreted as a mental shrug. '*If you don't wish to carry it, then place it on my tongue and I'll keep it safe within my mouth as we fly back.*'

Firestorm moved around and lowered his head until his lower jaw rested on the ground a few paces to Nolita's left. She flinched as he opened his mouth and pushed his tongue forward. To be this close to a dragon's open mouth, even if it was not angled towards her, caused the dark clouds of fear to boil up inside her mind again. She staggered slightly, as dizziness brought her to the brink of fainting. Grabbing the metal plinth on which the orb was mounted, she steadied herself, closed her eyes and drew in a deep breath.

On opening her eyes, she did not hesitate. In one swift movement, she reached out with her right hand, grabbed the orb with her fingertips and turned her palm upwards to support the crystal. The instant she did so, she realised that her forebodings had been correct. Where her fingertips held the orb she felt the strangest sensation, as if her fingers were being sucked in through the surface of the crystal.

She tried to return the orb to the plinth, but her hand could not release it. Pain erupted in her fingertips and she screamed aloud as hot spikes of lightning shot up her arm.

'*What is it, Nolita? What's happening? Put it down! Put it down!*' Firestorm's voice echoed loud in her mind, but she could not respond. Her eyes widened with horror as the first droplets of blood formed on her fingertips and trickled down the inner surface of the hollow orb, drawn by the fierce suction force. Even as she watched, the droplets began to collect at the base of the crystal. More blood followed, as the initial droplets became an increasing flow.

Panic overtook her. Still screaming, she staggered back from the plinth, the pooling blood sloshing around inside the orb. She grabbed her right wrist with her left hand and began to shake it with all her might, desperate to dislodge the leech-like globe of crystal. The consequences of breaking the orb if she dropped it did not enter her thinking. Pain and terror at what the orb was doing to her overruled all other thought.

'*Give it to me! Give it to me!*' Firestorm's voice in her head mirrored her panic.

For the first time since first encountering Firestorm she ran to him gladly. Her desperation to be rid of the orb momentarily enabled her to put aside her fear of the dragon and reach out to him for help.

'*Put it on my tongue,*' Firestorm ordered.

Without thinking, Nolita thrust her arm between the dragon's great jaws and placed the orb on Firestorm's tongue. The dragon flinched slightly at the contact, for no sooner did the orb touch him than it began to draw his blood as well. To Nolita's horror, however, no matter how hard she pulled, she could not release her fingers. Dragon blood was now bubbling in great quantity from Firestorm's tongue and mixing with the blood still flowing from her fingertips. The bright red rivulets were mixing and darkening as the orb slowly filled.

Was it her imagination? Was the orb growing? Would it keep sucking their blood until they were both empty husks of skin and bone?

Oh, gods, don't let it be so! she prayed, her mind shrieking with the pain in her hand. It was almost as if a line of fire was racing from her fingertips, up her arm and into her head. The burning terrified her. Pain had never frightened her before. She had always had a high tolerance to physical discomfort, but this sensation was different – almost alien in its origin. Was she now going to add another fear to her list?

'*It's slowing.*' Firestorm's voice in her head was calm now. '*Relax, dragonrider. You're not going to die.*'

He was right. The orb was almost full and the pain was receding.

'*I believe I understand the Oracle's riddle about this orb now,*' Firestorm added thoughtfully. '*Like all riddles, the meaning is obvious when you know the answer.*'

Nolita was intrigued, but the pain in her arm was still too distracting for her to want to know the answer. 'Save it,' she replied through gritted teeth, still straining to pull her hand free. 'The others will want to know too. You can tell us all together.'

As suddenly as it had held her, the orb let her fingers go. The abruptness of it caught her by surprise and she stumbled backwards. Before she realised what had happened, she was flat on her back and seeing stars from bumping her head on a lump of volcanic rock.

'Ow!' she said, gently probing the back of her head with the fingers of her left hand while flexing the painful fingers of her right. She sat up and checked herself over. The fingertips of her right hand were clean and undamaged. If it had not been for the orb full of blood resting on Firestorm's tongue, it would have been easy to conclude that the entire episode had been a waking nightmare. The back of her head felt tender, but there was no sign of bleeding there either. She had been lucky, she concluded, climbing gingerly to her feet.

Had she really just put her arm inside a dragon's mouth? It did not seem possible. Even the thought of such a thing was ridiculous.

The sound of Firestorm's laughter filled her mind. *'I doubt your brother or sister would be brave enough to do it,'* he said casually.

'Sable and Balard wouldn't be *stupid* enough to

get into a situation where they needed to,' Nolita answered. She laughed too, the nervous tightness in her throat causing her chuckle to squeak and crack. Her fear of Firestorm had lessened considerably. He still scared her, but the mindless fear that had paralysed her in the past had retreated. It was not gone, but she had defeated it to the point where she could keep the emotions under control.

Just as well, she thought, because I've still got to ride back.

It would be good to put it off further, but she knew that to do so would risk the return of previous levels of fear. Her mind and body had been subjected to so much terror during the past few minutes that if she was ever to be hardened to it, now was the time.

'Come on,' she said. 'We've got what we came for. Let's get back to the others and enjoy our moment of glory.'

Firestorm closed his mouth, the orb of blood still resting on his tongue.

'And be careful not to swallow that thing. I'm not going looking for another one,' she added.

'*As far as I know, there is no other*,' Firestorm replied.

'Then please try to resist any sudden urges to convert it into dragon poo!'

Firestorm snorted with amusement and tendrils of smoke curled from his nostrils.

Nolita climbed up onto Firestorm's back and settled into the saddle. She looked around. In a few heartbeats she would be airborne again. Despite feeling more comfortable in the dragon saddle, the familiar clamps of dread gripped her gut with their icy pressure.

'*Are you ready?*' Firestorm asked.

'No, but do it anyway,' Nolita answered aloud.

Firestorm did not need telling twice. He launched off the rim of the crater with a mighty leap, his great wings setting an urgent pace as they climbed back towards the higher peak that was home to the day dragon enclave. It was not a long flight back, but despite his excitement at their success, Firestorm took his time manoeuvring down into the crater that housed the entrance to the chamber of the Sun's Steps, keeping all his turns gentle and predictable for Nolita.

They landed gently to cheers even louder than the ones that had followed them when they left. Elian and Kira ran forwards to meet them. A large crowd of dragonriders, all cheering and clapping enthusiastically, followed closely behind them.

'Are you all right? Did you get it?' Elian asked breathlessly, his eyes wide with excitement as he looked up at her sitting on Firestorm's back.

'We're so proud of you, Nolita,' Kira interrupted before Nolita could answer. 'We both know how difficult that must have been for you today. Whether you got it or not, we're really proud.'

Nolita flipped her right leg over the pommel to join her left and slid down Firestorm's side onto his folded foreleg. Then she stepped forwards again and landed on the ground next to her companions. They both pulled her into a hug.

'Yes,' she said with a beaming smile as she returned their embrace. 'We got it – but the orb gave us a final surprise. It sucked our blood.'

'It did *what?*' Elian and Kira exclaimed in unison.

'Did you say "our blood"?' another voice interjected. It was Barnabas. The crowd of people around them parted respectfully to let the old dragonrider through. The three companions drew apart and turned to face him.

'Yes, sir. The orb sucked blood from both of us until it was full,' Nolita answered.

'Interesting! The records indicate that the previous two riders who won the orb could not break free from it until it was full of their blood, but neither mentioned it drawing blood from their dragon,' Barnabas said thoughtfully. 'I wonder . . .'

Then Firestorm's voice suddenly began chanting

in Nolita's head, blocking out everything else that was being said.

'*Delve 'neath the surface, life's transport hides,*
Healing, restoring – bright river tides.
Enter the sun's steps; shed no more tears.
Attain ye the orb; vanquish the fears.

'*The Oracle's words are clear now. "Life's transport" is blood. It hides beneath the surface of our skin. We also delved beneath the surface layer of the orb and hid blood within it – though it is hardly hidden, as the orb is transparent. And dragons have long identified that there are properties within blood that act to heal and restore our bodies when we are injured. We did enter the sun's steps; and you vanquished your fears. The verse all makes sense.*'

Nolita relayed his words to the others and they looked at her with a mixture of astonishment and respect. Elian's jaw literally dropped when Firestorm opened his mouth and Nolita stepped forward and reached between his rows of teeth to recover the orb from the dragon's tongue. She laughed as she saw his gaping mouth. It had been worth the wild surge of fear as she reached for the orb just to see Elian's face. Kira was beaming with approval too.

Barnabas stepped forwards and took the orb from her hands and held it up, examining it closely. After a moment he nodded and handed it back to her.

'You have done well, Nolita,' he said. 'Very well. But the three of you must now look to the future. The success of your quest hangs by a fragile thread. If it breaks, you will fail and all dragonkind will be ruined. Take this orb to the Oracle as fast as you can. The verse you quoted was different to those the Oracle gave to previous questors. Each time the Oracle has initiated the Great Quest the riddles have been different. Can you tell me the next verse?'

'*Release the dark orb – death brings me life.*

Take brave ones' counsel, 'ware ye the knife.

Exercise caution, stay pure and heed,

Yield unto justice: truth will succeed,' Nolita responded eagerly. 'Can you tell us what it means? Who are the brave ones? Is Pell right? Are they the leaders of the night dragon enclave?'

Barnabas closed his eyes for a moment, his lips moving slightly as he repeated the words of the verse over again. When he opened his eyes, his expression was more serious than ever.

'No, I do not believe that is the meaning of the verse,' he replied. 'If I'm not mistaken, the brave ones you should seek are the griffins. Before you begin your search for them, however, you must stop your companion, Pell, from reaching the night dragon enclave.'

'Why, sir?' Kira asked.

'The night dragons have always harboured an anarchic streak,' Barnabas explained. 'They have long felt restricted by the boundaries held in place by the Oracle. If they discover that the final attempt at the Great Quest has begun, they will likely see this as their chance to be rid of the Oracle. This will also provide an opportunity for them to dispose of the life purpose they have long held to be restrictive and troublesome. Without the Oracle's binding power to hold them in check, the night dragon enclave will likely move to seize power in every continent of the world. I doubt any could stand before them. Their strength and numbers are too great.'

'Then we should go – now!' Elian said, his impatient movement towards Ra matching the urgency in his voice. 'There's plenty of daylight left. We should use it.'

Kira nodded, but Nolita paled as she realised that she would have to climb into her saddle again. She felt emotionally exhausted, but knew that if she refused now, she might never do it again.

'Your backpacks are ready,' Barnabas told them, his face beaming as he gave each of them a brief hug goodbye. 'Nolita, you and Firestorm have honoured our enclave with your success. You will always be welcome here. We will pray good fortune for your quest. Good luck, riders.'

They grabbed their bags and climbed up into their saddles. Elian looked across at Nolita, who appeared as terrified as he had ever seen her. But she had mastered her fears. She was sitting on Firestorm's back. She was a proper dragonrider.

'Just let Pell try to mock her bravery again,' he said softly. With a final wave to the assembled day dragon enclave, he and Aurora powered into the air alongside Kira and Longfang. Firestorm paused a moment to give a roar of triumph, before carrying Nolita into the air behind them.

Here ends Book One of the Dragon Orb Quartet.

www.markrobsonauthor.com

DRAGON ORB: SHADOW

Book 2 in the fantasy series.

FOUR DRAGON RIDERS ON A MISSION TO SAVE THEIR WORLD

Pell and his night dragon Shadow must find the dark orb to help save the Oracle, leader of all dragonkind. But Segun, a power-hungry tyrant, stands in their way. Pell must use his flying skills, bravery and resourcefulness to the limit, as Segun is determined to get the orb - even if it means killing the opposition...

ISBN 978-1-84738-069-2

If you've enjoyed this series, you'll also like the
THE IMPERIAL TRILOGY
by Mark Robson

9781416901853   9781416901860   9781847380357

IMPERIAL ASSASSIN
"…a damn fine read … plenty of adventure,
fun and of course excitement." *Falcata Times*

IMPERIAL TRAITOR
"The Imperial series is a fine achievement."
Armadillo